"WHY ARE YOU HERE?"

"What?" Lucien dropped his hand to his side.

"Why are you here?" Adrienne demanded. "Escorting us home to Eynsham surely delayed you, if it didn't take you out of your way. You do appear to be on some sort of mission, either for your king or for yourself. Why, then, do you tarry at this humble keep?"

"I—" Lucien's black brows knit together above his nose as he frowned in consternation.

"Has it to do with your personal quest?"

"What!" It was his turn, now, to stiffen his shoulders.

"Is it a woman you're after?" Adrienne pressed. "Does she reside near here, perhaps at Cox or Widdenham? Is she some other man's wife?"

"Christ, no!"

"Then what possible reason could you have for remaining here when you had no intention of coming here in the first place?"

"You!" The syllable on his lips sounded more like a primitive growl than a recognizable word as he reached out again, this time with both hands and grabbing Adrienne's shoulders. As he drew her to him, he confessed, "I am here because of you!"

Dear Reader,

In July, we launched the Ballad line with four new series, and each month we'll present both new and continuing stories set everywhere from medieval England to the American West—the kind of passionate, romantic stories you love best, written by the most gifted authors. At the back of each book, we'll tell you when you can find subsequent books in the series that have captured your heart.

The pageantry of medieval England will sweep you away in **A Knight's Vow,** the first book in *The Kinsmen* series. In newcomer Candice Kohl's story, a dashing knight in search of vengeance finds a spirited woman instead—and passion in her embrace. Next, Gabrielle Anderson takes us back to early nineteenth century Boston with **A Matter of Convenience,** the first in a series in which three very special women find the men of their hearts' desire with the help of *The Destiny Coin.*

Mail-order brides don't expect romance—but that's what they'll find when they sign up with *The Happily Ever After Co.!* In Kate Donovan's first Ballad book, **Game of Hearts,** a woman dreaming of a better future will discover that a man from her past has the key to her heart. Finally, the second installment of Maria Greene's *Midnight Mask* series offers the magic of **A Lover's Kiss** when the infamous Midnight Bandit is unmasked by a woman who has nothing left to lose—and only love to gain in his arms. Enjoy!

Kate Duffy
Editorial Director

The Kinsmen

A KNIGHT'S VOW

Candice Kohl

Zebra Books
Kensington Publishing Corp.
http://www.zebrabooks.com

ZEBRA BOOKS are published by

Kensington Publishing Corp.
850 Third Avenue
New York, NY 10022

First Printing: September, 2000
10 9 8 7 6 5 4 3 2 1

Printed in the United States of America

*To my love, Sir Knight Philip of Brabant
who, alas, has no heritable lands*

Chapter 1

The South of England
Springtime, 1162

He saw the darker wench first. Lounging against a tree trunk, he took respite from the uncommonly hot morning sun by slaking his thirst with a cup of Fortengall Castle's finest brew, made from his mother's recipe, as he idly surveyed the crowd of fairgoers. He enjoyed a certain talent for spotting the comeliest wench in a crowd, be it in a humble village or at a banquet attended by King Henry's court. This girl caught his attention because she was so fine of form and feature that even her drab, peasant clothing could not dim her beauty. And, as was his habit, he amused himself by wondering who she might be: cottar's wife or freeman's daughter, married or maiden, virtuous or wanton.

He watched her speaking to someone blocked from his

view by the corner of a large vendors' tent. Now her arms went out, her hands disappearing behind the brightly colored fabric that billowed and rippled in the breeze. Unable to surmise what she was doing, he took a step away from the tree to alter the angle of his view. At that moment, *she* appeared.

Lucien went still, though he blinked rapidly, sure his vision had abruptly gone faulty. No maid, be she princess or peasant, could look as this one did.

The young woman appeared to be garbed in a hooded white cloak that glittered with threads of spun silver. Then she turned so she nearly faced him, and Lucien saw she wore only coarse tunics of faded blue and no hood at all. Her head remained bare, while the mantle draping her shoulders and flowing past her hips, nearly to her ankles, was the most glorious wealth of hair he had ever seen. Pale as moonlit snow, the sunlight rendered her tresses nearly blinding. And the face beneath it—

"Sweet Mother Mary!"

Lucien gulped the dregs in his cup before thoughtlessly tossing the empty vessel aside. Impatiently, he stepped to one side so that no passersby could obstruct his view. His continued perusal only confirmed his first impression. The girl was a beauty. She had a small, heart-shaped face, lush lips, rosy cheeks, and blue eyes. Cornflower blue eyes— startling eyes, not only because of their vivid hue but because they were framed by thick, sooty lashes. And above them arched a pair of fine, black eyebrows. All contrasted stunningly with the maiden's fair complexion and pale blonde mane.

"You ought not to unplait your hair," he overheard the dark-haired girl, the one Lucien had spied first, say. And stepping closer to better eavesdrop on their conversation, he finally saw what she'd been doing: running her fingers through the other girl's hair, using her nails to comb out the waves left by braiding.

" 'Tis unseemly," she added.

"It is not!" the fair beauty protested with a smile. "I've barely ten and eight years to my age, and I be a maiden in the bargain. There's no sin in letting my hair hang free."

"But . . . you've such a wealth of it!"

"Tsk, tsk, tsk," the blonde goddess responded before Lucien saw her wink impishly. "Don't behave like a stuffy old abbess, Lottie. You're no nun, and you're less than a twelve-month my elder. Besides, I only shook out my braids so that the hair ornaments I try on could be set off to full advantage."

While he continued to observe, the two young women stepped into the vendors' tent. With a slow, casual stride, he followed them and found them examining goods at an old woman's stall. The aged crone grinned as she set a circlet of flowers on the fair maid's head and began to fan out the long strips of embroidered cloth that flowed from it.

"God's tears, she's somehow made herself more beautiful," Lucien muttered to himself. On her, the chaplet of flowers with its many-hued ribands looked more dazzling than a crown studded with jewels. The colorful silk streamers against her shimmering tresses made the damsel stand out among the crush of peasants like a glittering gemstone nestled in a handful of rough pebbles.

While he watched, the maid twirled about and looked expectantly at the other girl.

"It certainly suits you, sister," the dark-haired girl admitted. "But the flowers will soon die."

"They're woven through grapevine," the vendor explained, "and may easily be replaced on a stroll through a meadow."

"But the cost!" she persisted. " 'Tis an extravagance to buy something so frivolous."

"What can you afford, mistress?" the woman asked the girl wearing the chaplet.

She responded by digging her slender fingers into the small leather pouch tied to her belt. Pulling out the contents, she displayed several short-cross pennies in her palm.

"This'll do," the woman declared, taking a few.

"Surely it's not enough!"

" 'Tis, if you pledge to tell all who admire that chaplet where it is you got it. I'll make up in extra custom what I lose on my sale to you."

"Truly?"

"Aye." She nodded, squeezing the maiden's pale fingers in her own spotted hand.

"My thanks, then. I vow to tell anyone who asks, and even those who do not!"

With a beaming smile, the blonde turned to the other damsel and said, "Let's hurry now. There's so much I would see and do before we join Wills to assist him at his stall."

After the girls set off together, Lucien approached the vendor's battered counter and announced without preamble, "I'll make up the difference."

The old woman squinted up at him. "That you, Lord Lucien? Lady Lucinda's son?" she asked, and he nodded. "Thought so." She turned her gaze toward the opening in the tent where the young women had exited. "D'you know her, the one with all that fine, white-gold hair?"

"Nay, not yet. But I intend to."

"Then go and seek her out. Don't worry about the cost of her trinket. I tell you truly, I'd have given it to her for the price of a smile. She's a grand one, she is, and probably the only one at the fair to do me work justice."

Undeterred, Lucien tossed a few coins onto the splintered board that served as the woman's trading counter.

"Do you know anything about her? Is she from the area—Tynsdale, Wexley, Kurth?"

"Can't say I've seen either of them before, milord. Her dress confirms her lowly station, but her looks . . ." The crone shrugged her stooped shoulders. "She must be a bastard sired on a local village wench by some fair-faced lord."

Lucien nodded thoughtfully. Certainly she was just that, the fruit of an intense passion between a peasant and her nobleman lover. He liked that romantic notion, and he savored it as he followed the path she had taken from the tent. He liked the idea so well, in fact, that he determined to continue the tradition with the girl herself.

Chapter 2

Lucien knew his way around a woman, whether he had already held her in his arms or had merely decided to seduce her. This one he observed cautiously, taking his time as he watched both girls tour the grounds obviously enjoying the jugglers, the musicians, and the food hawked, hot and steaming, by the local vendors.

As he critically contemplated the two young women, now engaged in earnest conversation with a bow-backed man selling metal wares, he noticed his brothers striding toward him. Each took one of his arms; flanking him, they said in unison, "Been looking everywhere for you!"

"Mother expects you to sup at the castle this eve," the raven-haired, black-eyed man on Lucien's right continued.

"Aye," the identical dark-haired young man on his left agreed. " 'Find Louie and bring him home for the evening meal. His little brothers are sorely missing him.' "

Lucien shook his head, shrugging Raven and Peter off.

"She'll never stop calling me that, will she?" he asked, expecting no reply. " 'Louie'—as if I were still a babe to be dandled on her knee."

Raven laughed good-naturedly. "Well, you know our mother. We will forever be her 'babes,' whether we're still wearing swaddling or we're balding and infirm."

Lucien nodded ruefully, stepping aside as a man led a horse along the path and headed toward the round pens at the far end of the grounds. As his brothers followed him, he observed, "It must be fine indeed to be the lords of Stonelee and Stoneweather. Nothing and no one to prevent you two from idling away a day at the fair."

Peter's gaze traced Lucien's. "I see you've wasted little time in finding a wench to pursue."

"Which?" Raven asked, as he, too, looked in the direction of the tinsmith's stall. When he spied the two young women at the booth, he asked, "Is it the maid with hair like soft mink, or the one with tresses the color of moonbeams?"

"Guess," Peter urged.

"Ah, the one who looks like an angel, of course." Raven folded his arms over his chest as the three of them boldly watched the young women slip beneath the counter board and begin assisting the stand's proprietor. "You've always been partial to blondes."

"Do either of you know her?" Lucien asked. "Have you ever seen her before?"

"No." Peter shook his head, his blue-black forelock falling into his eyes. As he raked back the offending hair with his fingers, he asked, "What's your plan, Lucien? She's a beauty, yet obviously a peasant. If you intended to dazzle her with your knightly presence, you ought to have garbed yourself in finer raiment."

"He's right," Raven agreed, looking Lucien over from head to toe. "With those short trousers, all you'd need is a cap to look like a bowman. Now Peter and I," he paused to preen a little, puffing out his well-muscled chest, "had the good sense to wear our finest tunics."

"Ah, but you're both landed lords," Lucien said, flashing a wry smile. "You've images and reputations to maintain. I, on the other hand, am naught but a knight in service."

"You could be landed as well," Peter pointed out.

"Aye. But with another man's lands. I want my own, those due me as my sire's heir. One day I'll have them. For now, I'll content myself with the knowledge that most lowborn females are impressed by knights-errant, while landed lords tend to overawe them."

"I won't argue the point," Raven said graciously, "though I could. The fact remains, Lucien, that today you look not at all the knight you are. At best, you could pass for a reeve or a warden."

"If the wench thinks me thus, or a serf or a servant, so much the better." Lucien's smile quirked jauntily, a wicked twinkle in his eye. "Methinks she'll be far easier to seduce if she believes me to be her equal rather than her better."

"Be prudent," Raven and Peter chorused. And Raven went on, "Should she discover you're a close relation to the earl of Fortengall himself, she may come running after you with a belly swollen out to here"—he gestured with both hands—"claiming the brat is yours. And you know Mother. Between her and Lord Ian, you'd have no choice but to marry the wench, even if the babe hatched as black as a Moor."

"I shouldn't think our elder brother would mind being wed to that particular wench, even if she's naught but a cottar's daughter. I know I shouldn't," Peter declared.

"God's teeth!" Lucien frowned. "I've yet to speak to the girl, and you have me siring her children."

"Well, go on, then," Raven urged, poking him in the

small of his back. "Speak to her. Peter and I shall come, too. If you make no headway with her, we'll advise you how to improve your suit later."

It was an old game the three brothers played. Many's the time they had wagered among themselves who would win which maiden during a leisurely evening of drinking and wenching. Frequently, one or the other would offer the third some whispered—or even shouted—advice on how to woo a girl targeted for attention. Thus, Lucien was not unduly annoyed by his younger brothers' presence. Yet he graced them both with a contemptuous look before sauntering off across the beaten path, leaving them to follow.

Fair-haired Adrienne saw the approach of the twin lords, both dark as devils, their clean-shaven faces as handsome as their saffron tunics were fine. Ahead of them strode a common man in simple garb. Nay. In the brief time it took him to reach the plank counter behind which she stood, Adrienne revised her original impression. The young man was anything but common—no grubbing farmer, he. Certainly a freeman who paid rents on his own property, or a servant in high esteem, possibly in service to one of the lords flanking him.

The raven-haired nobles fell back as they neared the tinsmith's stall, while the other fellow stepped forward and laid both his fists upon the counter.

"Aye, good sir. May I"—she cleared her throat—"help you?"

Adrienne clamped her lips closed, relieved she'd gotten out her question. Her throat had suddenly gone dry, and she felt a sheen of perspiration moistening the valley between her breasts. She knew that neither symptom was due to the warmth of the day and suspected—to her chagrin—they were precipitated by the presence of this stranger. A stranger, with a broad-shouldered, hard-mus-

cled body, hair the color of burnished copper streaked
gold by the sun, and eyes as green as emeralds.

"Aye, you may."

"What?" Flustered, her tongue tasting like parchment,
Adrienne swallowed hard.

"You asked if you could assist me. I certainly hope you
can."

"Oh. Yes."

Adrienne felt suddenly helpless, as though she'd just
fallen into a current destined to sweep her away, perhaps
even to drown her. Frantically she turned around, looking
for her sister to rescue her. She spied Charlotte at the rear
of the stall, so earnestly engaged in polishing a pewter
mug it seemed she was determined to make the dull metal
shine like pure silver.

"Mistress."

The stranger's voice compelled Adrienne to turn back
to him. Her lips parted as she wetted them, but no words
issued forth. The best she could manage was to raise her
winged black brows in mute question.

Lucien allowed his lips to curl up in an appreciative
smile. Damnation, the girl was exquisite! Delicate. Rare.
Like some exotic butterfly. And like any collector of butter-
flies, he was determined to possess this noteworthy spec-
imen.

From behind Lucien came sounds of exaggerated
coughing. It appeared that the lords of Stonelee and Stoneweather were choking, and it occurred to Lucien he would
find a great deal of pleasure wringing their necks. Instead,
he ignored his brothers and leaned casually on the splintered board separating him from the object of his desire.
In a low, caressing voice he explained, "I need a trinket."

"For what purpose? That is, 'twould help me to know.
So that I could select . . . you could choose . . ."

She fingered the plunging V-neckline of her bliaut nervously. Though beneath lay an under-tunic covering her to her throat, the girl might as well have begun to disrobe for him. Lucien's mind did it for her, stripping the faded layers of cloth from her bosom until her ruby-tipped, alabaster breasts were exposed, quivering in anticipation as they thrust forward, beckoning his touch.

A few moments passed before a loud, disdainful chortle—easily recognizable as his brother Raven's—forced Lucien to cease his musings. "I need a token," he explained. "A gift."

Adrienne's skin prickled. The man's voice tickled like a soft plume, stroking her, teasing her. She thought it might be wise to step away. Instead she moved closer, grateful that the counter board separated them.

"Could you, ah, tell me for whom?" She felt brazen asking, so she hurried on to explain, " 'Tis only that, if I knew, mayhap I'd be better able to—to show you something—appropriate. I shouldn't want to waste your time."

"Any time spent with you would ne'er be wasted."

A frisson of pleasure rippled through Adrienne's limbs, and her face warmed rosily. Spinning around, she gave the man her back as she tried to compose herself.

He was the one! He was exactly the sort she'd hoped to meet. 'Tis why she'd had the idea to go out into the world before her grandfather arranged marriages for herself and Charlotte. Before that day came, she wanted just once to know the attentions of a handsome young man and to experience love in his arms. Just one night with a virile swain who desired her for herself and not for what she might bring to him.

Stealing a brief glance at the attractive stranger, Adrienne assured herself that this encounter was ordained. The Fates themselves were responsible, just as they'd been responsible for her grandfather being absent from the keep when the traveling tinsmith, Wills, confided he was going to the earl of Fortengall's spring fair. Just, too, as they'd made the old peddler willing to take her and Charlotte with him, despite their being noblewomen—and unwed—with neither permission for the journey nor armed escort to protect them.

She couldn't let either her anxiety or inexperience be the cause of ruining this ripe moment, Adrienne decided. Yet when she spun around again, her anxiety abruptly returned. The stranger's gaze seared her, lingering hotly where it ought not to have, upon her bosom.

" 'Tis for a beautiful young woman," he announced, resuming their conversation.

"Oh?"

The single syllable sounded frosty to Adrienne's ears, as though she were a jealous lover—*his* jealous lover! She froze. With sudden insight, she knew she couldn't possibly be bold enough to take a lover. She would know no man except for her husband. Playing the brash vixen lay beyond even her inclinations, despite the fact that she was often described as too daring, too adventurous.

"Did you say something?" her customer asked.

"What? Nay." Adrienne shook her head vehemently, hoping she hadn't uttered her thoughts aloud. If only the man would make his purchase and leave!

Taking a deep breath, Adrienne pushed her long hair and ribands back over her shoulders. Grabbing a cooking vessel by its handle, she said, "I don't suppose she'd like a pot?"

"Would you like a pot?"

"No." Adrienne shook her head, dropping the pot onto the board with a clatter. "Candlesticks?" she suggested next, glad for a reason to look at something other than the man as she grabbed two pewter candlesticks and held them aloft, one in each hand.

He shook his head, crinkling his nose in distaste. "I think not."

Adrienne exhaled noisily and surveyed the length of the counter. There was naught on display that would suit as a gift for this man's lover—Adrienne was sure any beautiful young woman of his acquaintance was certainly his lover. "I must apologize, good sir," she explained, pinning her gaze on his nose rather than his eyes, lest she forget what she intended to say. "But the wares here are all rather practical in nature. I doubt you'd find anything to your liking."

"I must disagree." The fellow leaned forward, bringing his nose very close to Adrienne's so that she had to raise her eyes to prevent them from crossing. "I've already discovered something very much to my liking."

Adrienne's blood ran hot; she gripped the edge of the counter board to keep herself steady.

"What . . . would that be?"

He smiled, and it seemed he would whisper something in her ear. Instead he gestured to a cluster of figurines displayed at the end of the counter board. "These are rather well done," he said.

"Oh, aye, they are!" Adrienne lunged to the corner of the stall. "They are woodland creatures. Very skillfully crafted, wouldn't you say?"

She picked up one small animal to show him and inadvertently touched his hand. Adrienne felt a spark, like an ember from a hearth fire, and quickly pulled her hand away.

He grabbed her wrist and brought her hand back over the counter. When he rubbed his thumb over the soft skin just below her palm, Adrienne's pulse leapt. She knew he felt it, too, and feared he'd make some comment about her obvious distress. Yet he only said, "It appears to be a rabbit."

" 'Tis a hare, aye." Attempting to ignore the man's hand encircling her wrist, she looked down at the figurine she held. "See its nose? You'd almost expect it to twitch. And this one here," she added, picking up another with her free hand, "is a hawk."

"I see." Lucien released her with a lingeringly thoughtful look before glancing down at the remaining figurines. "A hare, a wolf, a hawk. What's this?" he asked, picking up another pewter figure. "It doesn't look like a woodland creature to my eye."

Though he'd asked her what the object was, instead of holding it out to her, he stepped away, feigning puzzlement as he studied the figurine. This forced the wench to lean well over the plank separating them as she craned her neck to better view the object Lucien was holding. The delightful—in Lucien's opinion—result was that her bosom rested on the wooden counter in the most delicious manner, as if she were serving it up to him on a trencher. A smug smile settled on his lips as he heard his brothers chuckling, ostensibly over some quip one or the other had made, but actually, he knew, in appreciation of this maneuver. Leaning forward at last, he brought his face very near the girl's once again.

"It is an angel," she announced. Her head snapped back though her eyes, round and startled, met his. "See the wings and the halo crowning her head? 'Tis an angel, that's what it is."

"I believe you're right," Lucien agreed, his eyebrow and the corner of his mouth quirking up simultaneously. It made his smile devilish, he knew, and seemed to cause the goose bumps that sprouted on the maid's arms. "Do you like it?" he asked her.

"Yes. I do. Very much."

She swallowed hard—Lucien saw her naked throat visibly constrict. He thought of pressing kisses there, and in the hollow at its base.

"I'll take them."

"Them?"

"All of them—the hare, the hawk, and the wolf. And the angel, of course."

"Oh! Very good."

Looking relieved to escape his presence for even a moment, she interrupted the tinsmith, who was haggling with another buyer. Lucien, meanwhile, stole a look over his shoulder. His brothers bowed and saluted, acknowledging his skill; he gave them a cocksure wink.

Adrienne returned. During her brief discussion with Wills, she'd regained her wits enough to know the turmoil she'd been experiencing had roiled only in her mind. The man—serf, servant, or freeman, whatever he was—had done naught to purposely stir her emotions. He had simply wandered by the stand and paused to make a purchase. When he had paid, he'd go, and she would never see him again. The Fates had not destined them to meet. She herself stood fully responsible, having nagged Charlotte into visiting the fair, dressing like a peasant, and assisting the tinsmith at his stall. When the episode reached its conclusion, Adrienne determined to stay close to her sister's side, return with her to their grandfather's keep, and dutifully do as she was bade for the rest of her days.

Lucien turned to face the maid as she named the peddler's price. Without haggling, he reached into his purse and pulled out several short-cross pennies. He did not count them, but held out his palm so that she might take them. Yet when she put her hand over his, about to close her fingers on the coins, he closed his fingers around her hand.

Holding her captive, Lucien looked deep into her eyes. "Will you meet me tonight?"

Adrienne froze. She had been counting the moments, expecting him to go from her life quickly. But he was not going. The Fates had, after all, maneuvered this meeting. She'd been arrogant to presume she had any control.

"Aye," she whispered, unable to answer otherwise.

"Where?"

She glanced fleetingly at Charlotte, who remained occupied in pulling Wills' handiwork from the barrels at the back of the fabric-draped stall. "We—my sister and I—will make camp with the other vendors when the fair closes this eve. I don't know—"

"I do. I'll find you."

With that promise, the stranger twisted his wrist, upended Adrienne's hand, and spilled the coins into her palm. Without turning and without counting them, Adrienne tossed the coins into Wills' money casket.

He scooped up the four figurines he had purchased. His large hand encompassed them all. "What are you called?" he inquired.

"Ad—Addy."

"Addy. This is for you." He plucked the pewter angel from his fist and handed it to her.

Adrienne stared at it as if it were the Holy Grail. "But—but you said—"

"I said 'twas for a beautiful young woman," he reminded her, "and so it is."

She felt her neck, her cheeks, and even her ears grow rosy with heat, but Adrienne made no attempt to hide her burning face. Instead she clutched the angel as though it could try to escape. Habit, more than cool reason, made her say, "Thank you . . . ?"

"Lucien. My name is Lucien. Remember it." With that, he gave her a wink that implied something already between them and hinted at more to come, before walking away with his purchases.

Adrienne watched him join the two dark lords who had remained a little distance from the stand as he, Lucien, made his purchase. She felt stunned that she'd agreed to meet him later, alone, after nightfall. It was one thing to fantasize about such a tryst; it was another to agree to one. Adrienne had absolutely no personal experience, but even she knew what happened when young ladies met men in the dark.

Yet she had agreed, and having done so, she felt no regret. Far from it, she felt a shiver of wicked anticipation at the prospect.

"Who was that?"

Turning to her sister, who had belatedly come to her side, she replied, "Lucien."

"Lucien! You know the man's name? I merely wondered what he was. He's dressed like a bowman, but he carries no quiver."

"You seemed to have observed him well, considering you did not come forward to assist me."

Charlotte's dark eyes went wide. "Addy, I didn't know you needed my help! You never seem to need my help, even when I insist that you do."

"Don't fret, Lottie." Adrienne patted her sister's shoulder. "I managed ... well enough." Her glance strayed from Charlotte's face to the place she'd last seen Lucien.

He was gone.

Falling in with his brothers, Lucien had already walked out of view of the tinsmith's stand.

"Damnably well done," Peter declared, chuckling and waggling his eyebrows.

"Aye," Raven agreed. "But all you've got to show for yourself is a pouch full of trinkets of which you've no need. If you'd gifted the wench with a miniver muff or a pearl ring instead of one of her own wares, she might have offered up her name, at least. Or better, some part of herself more intimate that a randy knave like you could truly enjoy."

Lucien smiled crookedly as he gave his brother a side-long glance. "Ah, you foolish lad. You didn't pay close enough attention, though I gave you a lesson well taught."

"What did I miss?" Raven asked as the three walked along together, their strides identical.

"I not only got the maid's name—Addy, if you would know—but I got her to offer up all she has to give, this eve, after the fair closes down."

The lords of Stonelee and Stoneweather whistled a single note duet. Then Peter clapped Lucien on the back. "God's bones, but you're damned skilled at wooing the wenches," he said appreciatively. "Raven here, who considers himself a lover extraordinaire, still cannot claim to be your equal."

"Well, I shall be," Raven chuckled, "or I'll swive myself to death trying!"

"Ah, that's the way for a knight to die," Lucien mused. "With his own weapon deep in a woman's sheath, instead of a foe's weapon deep in his gut!"

Chapter 3

Lucien strode into Fortengall Castle's great hall and found it occupied only by servants setting up the trestle tables for the evening meal. It seemed none of his family was present, until he heard high-pitched shouts from behind him:

"Lucien!"

"Lucien!"

"LUCIEN!"

He turned to spy his young half-brothers careening through the archway as they lunged at him and tackled his legs. He allowed them a minute of good-natured tussling before setting the eldest, Hugh, away and hoisting the twins, John and James, one under each arm.

"Have you brought us a token from your travels?" Hugh asked.

"A token from my travels!" Lucien repeated, putting

the four-year-olds down on their feet. "Mother must have you sitting with your tutor extra hours every day."

"Nay." The twin called James shook his head. " 'Tis only that Hugh thinks he's a great lord, like Father."

"Do not!" Hugh exclaimed, pushing at his little brother. Big-boned, fair-haired, and blue-eyed like his sire, he stood tall for his five years.

"Do, too!" the young twins sang in unison, and Lucien shook his head. Though they looked nothing like their older half-brothers, these carrot-topped, green-eyed twins already had the same habit of speaking as one.

"No squabbling, now," he told them, loosening the cord on his pouch. "As it happens, I do have something for you from the fair today."

"Mother wouldn't let us go again. She said we'd been there thrice already," James complained. "Why did you get to go?"

" 'Cause he's grown up and can do as he likes," Hugh informed his brother.

"Because I only just returned home," Lucien explained as he pulled the pewter figurines out and held them in his hand.

Squatting low so that the youngsters could better see, he plucked one decorative sculpture at a time from the palm of his hand. "This one's a hare, Jamie. 'Tis for you."

The little boy took it, his eyes widening with delight.

"This hawk is for you, John," he told James' look-alike, chuckling as the child grabbed it with his chubby, grubby fingers.

"And this is for you, the future Earl of Fortengall."

Hugh accepted the wolf graciously. "Thank you, Lucien," he murmured, his response quickly echoed by the twins. Next they were off, the three of them, up the keep's stairs, already squabbling heatedly over whose animal figure was superior.

For another few minutes, Lucien stood cooling his heels inside the hall. Idly he considered the chamber, deciding it truly deserved to be called a great hall because it was grand, indeed. Equal to many of the king's own. Yet even if he could call it his, Lucien knew he would not. The one he coveted was crude and cramped in comparison, but he wanted it with a passion.

"Louie?"

He turned toward the stairs at the sound of his mother's voice and discovered her hurrying down the steps, her husband ably guiding her with a firm hand on her elbow.

"I'm sorry. *Lucien,*" she corrected herself. "You know it has always been difficult for me to remember to use my sons' Christian names. Raven has completely abandoned the name he was given at birth. Methinks 'tis because of the damsels at court. 'Raven' is far more memorable to such ladies than the name I chose for him." She frowned and shook her head in exasperation as she came to a stop directly before Lucien.

"Raven does spend a great deal of time with the king and queen's entourage," Lucien agreed.

"That's true. But at least he's been playing dutiful Lord of Stonelee since Henry's been away in Anjou. Now you're here at Fortengall, too! But I hear you arrived yesterday, and I've not laid eyes on you 'til this moment. If the boys hadn't come to show us the figurines you'd given them, we'd not have known you were here, since you had no servant announce you."

"Good evening, Mother," Lucien said when Lucinda of Fortengall finally paused for breath. He smiled, genuinely pleased to see her. She remained a beautiful woman, with sparkling, emerald eyes and only a few threads of silver in her dark, cinnamon-colored braids.

"Lord Ian." Lucien gave a quick, respectful nod to his stepfather. The earl fairly dwarfed his wife. A big, blonde, well-muscled man marked by the scars of innumerable battles, he was known far and wide as The Dane.

"Glad to have you home again," the earl declared, a smile softening his scarred and bearded face as he clapped his eldest stepson firmly on the back. Together the three headed to the raised table at the far end of the hall.

"Surprised you managed the time to come here this eve."

Hearing the familiar voice chiding him, and realizing that both Raven and Peter were following, Lucien glanced over his shoulder, giving the pair a disdainful look.

"Have you plans, Lucien?" Lucinda asked as she mounted the dais and took a center chair beside her husband's.

"Nothing compelling," he replied, sitting next to her.

"I wouldn't wager on that." Raven grinned as he swung his leg over the empty chair at Lucien's side. "The wench looked quite compelling when we saw her today at the fair."

"Were you ogling the young ladies there?" Lucinda frowned her disapproval at her grown twin sons.

"Not us!" the two dark lords insisted, their voices raised in unison. "In truth," Peter elaborated, " 'twas your eldest who did all the ogling. *More* than ogling, if you need know."

"Mother needn't know," Lucien said tersely, a raised eyebrow silencing not only Peter but Raven, too.

The meal commenced, and the family discussed family matters—Fortengall, Lucinda's dowerland of Tysdale, and the twins' adjoining baronies, Stonelee and Stoneweather. They also discussed Lucien's recent months in service to the king. Occasionally Lucien glanced toward the sliver of sky visible at the top of the hall's narrow arrow slits. But night had not yet fallen. The advancing spring had lengthened the days, so he knew he had ample time yet before he was due to seek out Addy.

"Lucien," the earl addressed him.

"Aye, my lord?"

The big man leaned on the table with his forearms, peering around his wife. "I would speak with you about the matter of your quest."

Inwardly, the young knight sighed. *He* had no wish to speak of his seemingly vain and futile quest. Years past, when he and his brothers had fought at King Henry's side, helping the young monarch to rid England of some particularly loathesome barons, he could have accepted the king's offer of a large parcel of confiscated land. Peter and Raven had, carving one estate into two and building twin keeps almost side by side. But Lucien had declined Henry's generous offer. At the time, he believed he would swiftly take back the land that was rightfully his as eldest son to Gundulf of Eynsham. But he'd made little enough progress in the past six years, and Lucien doubted he would make much more in the next six. Politely, though, he responded, "What is it you wish to know?"

"About your men," Lord Ian said simply. "If you suddenly had the means to pay them, could you recruit enough men for an army to make your attack?"

Lucien sat sideways in his chair so that he better faced his stepfather. "Aye," he replied slowly. "Not that such a miracle would e'er occur. But should it, I could mount a large enough force. Besides the knights from Fortengall you've offered me, and my brothers and their guards, Harold of Becknock, the lord we fostered with, has agreed to lend me some of his own men-at-arms. Yet as you well know," he continued with a self-deprecating grin, "none owe me allegiance, so all must be compensated. As I've no more wealth than any knight-errant, I cannot pay them. Thus, it matters not how many I could recruit."

Lord Ian nodded thoughtfully. "In the years since you lost your heritable lands to your father's cousin, Osric," he said, "you have served both me and King Henry. I understand your situation, Lucien, for I once did the same. Born my sire's fifth son, I would never have been named Earl of Fortengall if all who came before me had not died.

"But you," he pointed out, tenting his fingers beneath his bearded chin, "were born the eldest in your house. You should be lord of your sire's estate."

"Another moot point," Lucien said evenly. "As that humble demesne was stolen from me the moment my father, Gundulf, drew his last breath, it seems unlikely I shall ever rule there as its lord."

"You're not giving up?" Peter asked seriously.

Lucien turned to him. "Nay, of course I shan't give up. But it took Osric a score and five years to lead an attack on Eynsham Keep, and I am resigned to the fact it shall most likely take me just as long."

Lucinda placed her hand over her son's, and Lucien turned his head toward her. He found her looking aside, at her husband.

"May I tell him?" she asked Lord Ian. When he nodded, she looked again at her eldest. "Lucien," she began, "a messenger from Henry and Eleanor arrived at Fortengall this very morn. He brought word and a cache of valuables. Henry's message is that he thinks it high time you took back what is yours. The gold and jewels are to help you do it."

"What!" Lucien glanced from his mother to his stepfather, then over to the twins. "Henry said naught of this to me before I took my leave of him so recently."

"Mayhap our dear queen persuaded him," Lucinda suggested.

Lucien shook his head bemusedly. "The king and queen are funding my army?" he asked, needing confirmation.

"Not quite," Lord Ian explained, a wry smile on his lips. "Our monarch may rule the largest kingdom in history, but he's still close with a coin. Henry, as a rule, repays his debts, though, and he remains beholden to you. Because you declined the land your brothers accepted after you three did him such good service, the king is now willing to aid you in getting back your birthright. However, Henry's not generous enough to finance the entire venture.

"So I am adding to the pot," the earl declared, "for you've done me fine service as well during these years I've been wedded to your mother. Between us, Lucien, you should have enough coin to compensate any mercenaries you'll need. Providing," he added, "you make quick work of the whoreson who is living in your keep."

Rarely did Lucien fall speechless; this time was one. Staring openmouthed at his family, he could do naught but slowly shake his head.

"It's true." Raven grinned, nodding his head in counterpoint to Lucien's. "Now the money as well as the men are within your means. Lucien, there's nothing standing in your way." He clapped his brother on the shoulder. "You can take back Eynsham. You *will* take it back."

"By the blood of Christ, you know I will!" Finding his voice again, Lucien's full lips curled in a confident grin, and his slanted eyes flashed.

"I know you must do it," Lucinda said in a small voice, "though the thought of my three eldest sons all going into battle together is more than I can bear."

"Mother." Lucien kissed her temple as he rose from his chair. "Always you've worried over our safety. Yet always we've returned from battle unscathed. Mayhap it is your worrying that protects us, so do not cease. But rest assured we shall all emerge victorious from this fight."

"A toast to Sir Lucien!" Raven declared, standing and hefting his wine goblet as he thrust Lucien's own into his brother's hand.

"Nay," Peter countered, rising with Lord Ian to join

the other two on their feet. "A toast to Lord Lucien—of Eynsham, once again!"

It was light in the field where Fortengall Fair had been held. A great, white moon, a vast array of pulsing stars, and a huge bonfire pushed away the darkness.

Charlotte and Adrienne sat on a log at the perimeter of the peddlers' camp. Before them lay the open field and the blazing fire; behind them, the vendors' wagons were clustered haphazardly. Between them, stretched out on the ground with his head propped against the rotting trunk, Wills slept soundly.

Charlotte turned to her sister and said, "I've never before seen a night so brightly lit."

"This is what it must be like to travel with minstrels or mummers," Adrienne decided, glad she could think of anything at all to say to Charlotte. Despite her foot tapping to the music men played on pipes and strings, her mind was not at all on the merrymaking. She could only think of Lucien and the passing time that brought him closer to her.

"Is this night adventure enough for you?"

"What!" Adrienne snapped, turning to face Charlotte. Then, dropping her voice, she asked guiltily, "What adventure is it you think I've planned for this night?"

The other girl's fine, dark brows knit in a frown. "Addy, I didn't say I thought you had some new adventure planned. I hoped that this"—she gestured with a sweep of her arm to the bonfire, the musicians, the dancers— "had proved the adventure you sought when you wheedled Wills into bringing you here and me into coming along. Is it? Is it what you'd imagined?"

Exhaling a loud sigh, Adrienne nodded. "Oh, aye," she said. "More than."

Still frowning, Charlotte scooted closer to Adrienne. Now Wills' head was nearer to her feet. "Addy, are you well? You've seemed . . . queer . . . all this afternoon."

"Queer!" Adrienne feigned offense. "I've not been acting queer." She turned away and hugged her knees, trying to still their damnable bouncing. She was glad for the wealth of her skirts, which helped to hide her uncontrollable, nervous jiggling. " 'Tis only," she went on with a shrug of her shoulders, "that the fair has been so exciting. I've been caught up by it. Distracted."

"I think that man, Lucien, is the one who distracted you."

Adrienne swallowed hard, too cowardly to face Charlotte again. It surprised her whenever it happened, when Lottie—who was not only as dark as Adrienne was fair, but as quiet as she was lively, as cautious as she was reckless—read her so keenly. As though she, Adrienne, were a piece of parchment lined with inked script.

Yet she would not admit that Charlotte's suspicions were true. And as she could not get her knees to stop bobbing either, Adrienne leapt to her feet. "Dance with me," she urged, holding her hands out. " 'Tis a waste to let this fine music float over our heads without dancing to it."

"I don't dance well, and you know it."

"What difference?" Adrienne grabbed her sister's hand and hauled her up. "You're not at the king and queen's court. No one who might see you here even knows who you are." She pulled on Charlotte's arm, dragging her nearer to the fire and the other dancers. "Look at those drunken fellows!" Adrienne pointed to several who were stumbling and tripping, yet laughing all the while. "If they think that is dancing, you've naught to worry about!"

Even Charlotte could not deny it, so, with a smile, she attempted to follow Adrienne's frantic footwork.

And frantic it was, for Adrienne was deseperate to occupy

her mind with something other than thoughts of the stranger and what she had all but promised him.

"Oh, Addy, stop! Please!" Charlotte begged after a while. Her face was flushed and her brown eyes sparkling. "I had little rest during the three days we spent on the road, what with the night sounds that kept me awake, wondering at their sources. Now you've worn me out completely." She took a deep breath as she freed her hands from Adrienne's. "Methinks I'd best return to Wills' wagon and get some sleep while I can."

"So soon?"

"Aye. But it's not so soon," Charlotte added, nodding toward a number of others who were making their way to their own pallets. "Besides, we'll be up very early to begin the journey home. You should come, too."

"Dance with me, mistress?"

Adrienne spun around and saw a young, pimply-faced youth. She recalled seeing him earlier, selling fried honey cakes at the fair. "Aye," she agreed before turning back to her sister. "You don't mind, do you? I—I'm not tired, yet."

"Don't be too long," Charlotte cautioned as she headed in the direction of Wills' dray. "Dawn will come quicker than you know."

And Lucien will be here long before that. Adrienne shuddered, unnerved by a mix of emotions—fear, excitement, and trepidation. Then the youth grabbed her hand, and she gladly abandoned her misgivings in favor of enjoying the merriment swirling all about her.

Lucien remained at the castle. Upon learning his dreams were within his reach, his quest soon to be met and vengeance finally his, he, his brothers, and the earl had begun some serious celebrating. It had not all been boastful toasts and bold predictions, but such had made up most of their conversation.

Boasting and predicting proved thirsty work. They'd drunk everything they could lay to hand—strong wine, heady beer, sweet mead. During their discourse, the others had grown lethargic, their thoughts and their words straying to other topics. But Lucien's mind remained filled only with thoughts of his father's cousin, Osric, the man who had cost him his birthright. The fantasies he conjured, images of how he would lay low his enemy, seemed clearer and more satisfying now that they approached reality.

Exhilarated, Lucien did not grow drowsy. "Jesu," he muttered, glancing at his dozing companions sprawled in their chairs at the table, all of them snorting and snoring. "Go to bed, the lot of you," he ordered as he came to his feet.

Yet none of them moved from their chairs; in fact, none even stirred when Lucien stomped his feet on the dais to get the blood flowing to his legs again.

"Mother won't like this," he warned softly as he left them, secretly pleased that he would be spared Lady Lucinda's wrath when she came downstairs to collect her husband and found her sons in their cups as well.

Encountering a serving wench as he left the hall, he gave her a lewd smile wondering, vaguely, if he could entice the girl upstairs to his chamber. God knew, he needed a woman.

"A woman!" he gasped as the wench passed him by and he lost the opportunity. "Addy!" he mumbled, abruptly recalling their assignation. Lucien hurried down the corridor, ignoring the guards at the front portal, and yanked open the heavy-timbered, steel-banded door.

It was night, and from the looks of it, it had been night for some while.

Adrienne again sat on the log. Wills still slept soundly, snoring loudly, on the ground beside her. It seemed, as she gazed out across the Fortengall meadow where the fair vendors had made their camp, that nearly everyone else was asleep now, too. Silence had replaced the merry music, and even the fire burned low. She appeared to be the only waking sentry.

The woods encroached on this edge of the meadow not too many paces from the log on which she sat. Adrienne's eyes kept grazing the line of trees, hoping she would see Lucien stepping out from them. But she did not see him; he did not come.

She felt a little furious that he would toy with her in such a fashion. She felt a little hurt, for she'd believed him when he'd said he would find her. She was also embarrassed by her own careless vow to meet with him, a stranger. But above all else, Adrienne felt relieved. She would not now be forced to face the consequences of her foolish indiscretion, and none save she would be aware either of her impulsiveness or her subsequent humiliation.

It was best this way, she told herself as she hugged her knees and shivered in the damp, night air. Fortengall Fair itself had been enough of an adventure. She needed no handsome stranger to flatter her with compliments or steal kisses from her in the dark. Nay, the fair had been enough. Now she could return home and submit to marriage with whomever her grandfather chose. She would be satisfied, having had this one little adventure.

Adrienne's eyes made another sweep of the dismantled fairgrounds, the peddlers' camp, and the stand of trees nearby. She knew she should rise, walk to the dray, and climb into the straw beside her sleeping sister.

But she could not do it. Not yet. Not for a little while. Later, she would go. Later, she would burrow into the hay beneath the rough blankets and sleep 'til sunrise. But it was not so very late yet. She would tarry just a bit longer.

Chapter 4

He moved so soundlessly though the grass, Adrienne gave a little start when she suddenly discovered him standing nearby, his hand held out to her beckoningly. She might have hesitated, but he seemed almost magical, as if he had materialized in the moonlight. With a fluid movement, she laid her hand in his. Lucien urged her up, and as though in a dream, she floated along beside him.

He led her into the woods, not very far, but far enough so that the remains of the fairgrounds, the peddlers' ragtag camp, and even Fortengall Castle might have been leagues away instead of only paces. Adrienne found herself as alone with Lucien as if they were God's first people in the Garden.

She would have spoken, but his mouth came down upon hers in a bruising, hungry kiss that drew her so deeply she all but drowned in it. When Lucien's tongue explored her mouth as though it had a right to, Adrienne tried to resist.

A voice that often piped up from the back of her mind screeched its warnings: she was a lady, he was no lord; she was a virgin, he was a knave; she had put herself in a vulnerable spot, he would use her naivete to his advantage.

But, as she frequently did, Adrienne ignored the voice in her head until it grew fainter and fainter, finally fading away altogether. As she squelched her conscience, her good judgment and her reason, she gave herself up to the moment—and the moment was magical. Though the night air was cool, its crispness had a scent sweet and fragrant; it smelled of dark, damp earth and pungent pine. It also smelled of Lucien: leather and musk, tangy, fermented spirits, and damp, human heat. All of the scents, swirling together, intoxicated Adrienne, so she surrendered herself to the moment as people forced to ford an icy stream will plunge into the water—totally, quickly, completely.

With a moan deep in her throat, she leaned into Lucien. While he held her more surely, his hands roaming her curves, she pressed his tongue back with her own, licking his hot lips, skimming his smooth teeth. When he grabbed a fistful of her satiny tresses and ribands in his fists, exposing her small ear to his caresses, Adrienne quivered within his fierce embrace. Yet she found the hollow of his throat and dared to press soft kisses there until, leaving a trail of heat across his corded neck, she felt his life's blood pulsing. There she branded him with her lips, clinging to him all the more fiercely as she felt her legs losing their strength.

Adrienne did not crumple, yet her clothes fell away. She felt no cold embracing her limbs, only her lover's hot hands as they raked her back, kneaded her breasts, cupped and squeezed her bottom. The feel of his fingers, his lips, made her want more of his touch. Soon she was scrabbling at Lucien's clothes, enduring the abrupt and intolerable loss of his stroking for some moments as she impatiently tugged his shirt over his head and eased down his short pants, his leggings, and his braies.

Again she was back in his arms, her peaked breasts pillowed against the broad expanse of his smooth chest, his manhood nestled hard against the swell of her naked belly. Adrienne's flowered chaplet was lost among the ferns on the forest floor as she tossed back her head and shook her mane like a frisky mare with the scent of a stallion in her nostrils.

The heat was in her, burning in its intensity, overwhelming in its newness and unexpectedness. It made her bold and daring, as Adrienne found herself imitating Lucien—stroking, exploring, savoring the feel of her first, and certainly only, lover's flesh. She splayed out her fingers upon his bared back and memorized the contours and expanse of it; she traced the narrow hollow that cleaved his broad chest in two. She cupped his buttocks in her palms, kneading the tight muscles, and brought her hands around his narrow hips until they met in a nest of manly hair. While her lips were still joined to his, she moved her hands up between their straining bodies, hefting the weight of his heavy cod in one hand while she explored the length of his root by grasping it near his groin. Gently she pulled on it until its smooth head was cupped within her hand.

Lucien groaned and went down on his knees, taking Adrienne with him. He pushed her down before him, tumbling after her, seeking one nipple with his lips. She spread her thighs to soften his descent as he lay against her, but there was nothing he could do to smooth the rough pallet on which she lay. Nature had provided a bed of moss and pine straw, but the earth was hard and uneven.

Adrienne was oblivious to any earthly discomforts. Her mind subservient to her body, she instinctively arched toward Lucien, wriggling her hips and thrusting against him.

Seeking to solace her neglected breast, he smothered a cry deep in his throat as he felt her tuft of silken maiden hair tickle his belly. Making sounds that bespoke more of pain than pleasure, he forced himself up. Looking down at her pale skin lighted only by the firmament peeking through the leafy canopy above, he cupped her woman's flesh and slid two fingers between its slick folds.

The girl cried out. Not ceasing for a second his expert stroking of the swollen nub secreted between her ivory thighs, Lucien lay down beside her, kissing her hard to swallow her cries and hold the silence undisturbed. When she squirmed, he doubted she understood her own carnal cravings. But he fed them unabatedly until she writhed and spasmed with her climax. Then Lucien half sat and gathered Addy to him, hushing her wordless love cries by pressing her face into his shoulder.

She was glistening with perspiration when he laid her back down again. Yet she licked her parched lips invitingly and gazed up at him with such unabashed trust in her bright, black-lashed eyes, it was all Lucien could do not to spend himself like an untried youth upon the leaves he was crushing with his knees. Quickly he urged her thighs farther apart; with a tentative thrust, he placed himself in her.

Adrienne's blue eyes widened farther, and Lucien felt her tense. Yet when he put himself over her, his body a tent blocking the starlight and casting his flushed face in shadow, she relaxed again.

Slowly he eased himself nearly all the way out of her tight, virgin sheath. Then again he moved cautiously back inside that sweet, secret place of hers that hugged his manhood as if it had been fitted to size—this time just a bit farther. Again he moved out and again he moved in, while the woman beneath him closed her eyes dreamily and rested her hands confidently on his shoulders. But when, at last, he pushed his shaft to its full length, breaching as he did so the thin barrier that had kept him tentatively at bay, Adrienne's eyes flew open. Her mouth went wide, too, as she gasped in surprise and a tear of betrayal streamed down one cheek.

Lucien might have felt guilty for not warning her, but his own pleasure in her was so exquisite there was no room in his heart for regret. Raining tender kisses on her eyes, forcing them closed again, her thick, damp lashes resting heavy on the curve of her cheeks, he resumed his rhythmic thrusting. Though he feared Addy might recoil and try, vainly, to free herself from his invasion, she did not. In moments her own rhythmic thrusting matched his. And as their primitive mating dance increased its pace, growing more frenzied as they rushed, headlong, toward the precipice of their passions, Adrienne twined her legs about Lucien's waist, cleaving him to her.

Thus they were wrapped about each other as the knight found release in his lady's arms, and she, for a second time, knew the thrill of erotic abandon. They stayed entwined for long minutes after each was sated, inhaling the other's musky scent and tasting the salt on their skin as they nestled together in their forest bed.

Lucien frowned into the darkness. He and Addy were snuggled into a nest of their discarded clothing; still as nude as he, she nestled against his side as though her figure had been fashioned to fit his frame. It was perfect, she was perfect—with this minx he'd experienced the finest coupling of his life. By all rights, he should have been contemplating the boasts with which he would regale his brothers: Addy's attributes, her innate enthusiasm, her instinctive skill. But he was not thinking of such things, for he knew he would never speak of this maid in crude terms to anyone, least of all Raven and Peter.

Despite the fact that she lay as still as a sleeper, Adrienne was very much awake. Now that she had experienced romantic passion, her conscience again began to nag. She ought not to have come here, to the fair or this tryst. Despite their intimacies, Lucien remained a stranger still. Certainly she should never have given herself to him so completely, so freely. He was not her husband nor could he ever be, for she outranked him in heritage and title. Lucien could be only one thing to Adrienne—forbidden.

And yet . . . this had not been her doing. If anyone was to blame, it was the Fates. How could a mere mortal woman defy the Fates? Why would she even want to? Making love with Lucien had been wonderful, enchanted, glorious.

Adrienne felt like Eve, who had tasted the forbidden apple and enjoyed the fruit. But unlike Eve, she felt little shame or guilt now that the deed was done. If it were always thus between men and women, she finally understood why love—not survival, or wealth, or even allegiances sworn to God and kings—motivated mankind. The revelation was profound, and Adrienne understood the insight was denied to all virgins. She was glad, then, to be one no longer.

"Where is your home, Addy?"

Lucien's voice startled her; his question made her wince. She wished she owned special powers, like the pixies, fairies, and witches who lived in these same woods. Then she might disappear, leaving Lucien to wonder if he'd ever known her. But she was not a fey creature. She was solid flesh and bone, and Lucien clasped her to him. There was no way to avoid answering his query, though she determined not to tell him the whole truth. He had no need to know all of it.

"Some leagues distant," she replied, turning her face in the crook of his arm so that she could better see his rugged profile. "I live with my grandfather and my sister."

"The dark-haired damsel."

"Aye. Lottie. She's my senior by less than a year."

"And the peddler? Is he your grandsire?"

Adrienne imagined that and laughed. "Oh, no." She shook her head in the pillow of Lucien's arm. "The tinsmith's name is Wills. He oft repairs pots and sells his metal wares in our district. When he confided his plans to catch the last day of Fortengall's Fair, I begged him to take us with him. And he did, so here we be."

"Your grandsire did not object?" Lucien asked dubiously.

"Nay. But then he wasn't home and we could not tell him, so he does not know."

She giggled again, and Lucien thought of bells—light, clear-noted bells.

"Where do you live?" she asked him.

"Here in this shire, when I'm home. Which is rare enough."

"What sets you to traveling?"

Lucien scowled and, knowing he was scowling, glanced away. It seemed, indeed, all too decidedly perfect. Too damnably perfect. The wench, their tryst in the woods. Naught could be so perfect unless, perhaps, it had been arranged.

He glanced sidelong at Adrienne again. Though he discovered her eyes contentedly closed, he thought what he always thought when strangers probed him with personal questions: perhaps Osric had sent them.

"Why do you ask?. he demanded, his tone more short than he'd intended.

"I didn't mean to pry." Her eyes flew open, and she raised herself up on her forearm. "I should probably go now, before Lottie awakens and discovers me missing."

"Nay." He tugged on Adrienne's arm, forcing her back against his length. The curve of her cheek and her breast seemed designed to press against him, and he stroked her silvery hair in an attempt to hold her there.

Lucien chided himself for his foolish suspicions. If Addy were a courtesan or a baron's daughter, aye, then he might have sound reason to suspect she had ties to the self-proclaimed Osric of Eynsham. But she was nothing more than what she seemed, an unspoiled—'til recently—village girl. Only his sudden wealth and escalating plans for revenge made him doubt the innocence of their encounter. Besides, to Lucien's knowledge, his old enemy had never sought word on his whereabouts or plans. No doubt Osric considered him of no consequence. It would prove a fatal mistake.

He smiled when he looked again at Addy. Obviously her queries had only been an attempt at making conversation. That was a fault of every freshly bedded female, for none could roll over and fall asleep as any satisfied male could do.

She had a flaw! With a growing sense of ease, Lucien realized that this exquisite, naked woman beside him wasn't quite so perfect after all.

"Once," he said slowly, at last responding to Adrienne's question, "someone stole from me that which is mine. Everything I do is in my quest to win it back."

His answer surprised her and made her wonder what valuable a man of his humble means might have owned. A jewel? A purse of coins? A holy relic? A—woman?

The thought of another woman pricked Adrienne sorely. It wasn't right. She should not have such intense feelings for him. Men did this sort of thing with all manner of women. Why couldn't a woman do it, even once, without bruising her heart?

Stifling a sigh, she looked up, away, and determined not to regret this incredible night.

"What are you looking at?" Lucien asked gently, noticing Adrienne's eyes had fastened on the bit of night sky visible directly overhead.

"The stars," she told him on a sigh. "Our destinies are written there, did you not know?"

"Nay, I did not know." Lucien smiled indulgently. "Can you read my future in the stars?"

"I was thinking I wished that I could, so that you might know if you would one day be successful in your quest. Alas, I cannot. Nor can I read mine, either. I know only the Fates plot out our lives and write it in the heavens. Those wise enough to decipher what is written there can know the future. But I am not that wise."

Adrienne sat up, drawing her knees to her chest and hugging her legs with her arms. Though naked as a nymph, she was demurely covered. "Do you worry that you'll fail to retrieve what was stolen from you?"

"I shall retrieve it," Lucien assured her. "In fact, this very eve at my mother's table, I learned there are those who would assist me."

"That's good news!" She smiled at him warmly as she shook her head, swinging her thick veil of glossy hair over her arms and legs. "Will you soon be off and journeying again?"

More of Adrienne's back than front was visible to Lucien. Reaching up, he began tracing the length of her spine from her neck to the cleavage at the top of her derriere. "Aye," he sighed distractedly, "I will be off again very soon."

Adrienne tried not to shiver as Lucien's touch sent little sparks skittering not only across her back, but across her breasts and belly, too. Inhaling a deep breath, she tried to continue their conversation. "Will you be traveling across England, or heading to Normandy or Germany or some other wondrous place?"

"What makes you think them wondrous?" Lucien chuckled, his fingertip outlining images of flowers and birds on the canvas of Adrienne's back.

"Because I've never been to foreign lands and doubt I ever shall. Not even those our good king rules."

"I've been there, and take my word, Addy, though some places have their own allure, none can compare with England and what's to be found here."

Lucien sat up, and his single finger was joined by the rest as his hand roamed from Adrienne's back to her side to her breast. When he cupped the weight of her breast gently in his palm, she leaned against him.

Adrienne realized he had not really answered her question. She surmised he had a secret he'd no wish to share. She could not fault him for it; she had her own secrets. Soon enough—when she returned home to pose as a virgin bride for some yet-to-be-named husband—Lucien and this night they were sharing would be one of those secrets.

His lips were moist against her shoulder as his hand roamed down her belly to finally urge her closed thighs apart. "You're thinking," he murmured. " 'Tis a dangerous thing for a woman to think."

She opened her legs to his questing fingers. "I am not," she vowed as she tilted her head so that he could better kiss her neck and her shoulder. It was not a lie, because Adrienne's senses consumed her; all thoughts were pushed aside. The only thing she knew was Lucien's touch as he rekindled in her loins the flames he alone could put out.

Lucien stoked those flames to a white hot heat. Containing the passionate inferno that engulfed the two of them nearly undid him.

* * *

It was nearer tomorrow's dawn that yesterday's sunset when Lucien and Adrienne stepped out of the woods. The huge bonfire the merchants had built after the fairgoers departed was nothing now but glowing orange embers scorching the ground. Lucien led Adrienne closer to it.

"No farther," she whispered, halting him by placing her palm on his chest. "Our dray is right there. Wills is even still sleeping where I left him."

"And just as loudly."

They laughed at the peddler's sonorous snoring before Lucien pulled Adrienne into his arms and kissed her long and hard a final time. He felt some urgency, a need to put his mark on her, as though his lips bore his own seal and Adrienne's were soft, warm wax.

Knowing this to be their last kiss ever, she intended to memorize the smallest detail. She would treasure the memory, hoard it, and take it out to savor again and again.

The kiss burned so intensely that when it ended, they both felt bereft. Each stood stiffly, facing the other. Lucien stared at Adrienne, but she, unable to look into the depth of those fathomless green eyes of his without risking drowning in them again, looked heavenward instead.

"The stars are fading," she announced softly. "Even could I have read them, they are lost to us now."

" 'Tis probably best we mortals cannot see our futures," Lucien declared solemnly. His face then split with a smile. "But I know yours, if you don't get into that wagon before your sister wakes."

"Oh?" Adrienne purposely tried to sound carefree. "What will become of me if Lottie discovers I've spent the night with a man I only met yesterday?"

"She'll hold it over your head, threatening to tell your grandsire. To keep her mouth shut, you'll be forced to do all her chores as well as your own—milking the cow, slopping the pigs, churning the butter, sweeping the hearth . . ."

Lucien's list went on and on, until Adrienne really did laugh aloud. She tried to imagine her grandfather having her and Lottie do such chores. It nearly made her laugh again.

"As dawn shan't be long in breaking," she said with a smile, "you'd best be returning home, too. No doubt the lord who employs you will expect a good day's service come the morn."

Lucien nodded, but he was thinking how good it felt to have no lord to serve, not the earl nor even the king. From this day on, he was his own master.

"Farewell," he whispered, squeezing her hand. Adrienne turned then, and he watched her until she climbed into the back of a long cart and disappeared behind its slatted sides.

Jesu! he thought as he retraced his steps through the woods he knew so well. If only he were whatever it was Addy thought him to be. He'd like her swollen, shaped like a pear, big with his babe. He'd wed her, too, having no other cares.

But he was no villein. He didn't coax his living from the land, or serve some baron as a craftsman or laborer. Firstborn son of a lord and lady, his only objective now lay in securing his birthright, which had been stolen from him. He had not the luxury of taking a woman to wife. Hell, he hadn't even the time to enjoy a mistress, no matter how high or low her station.

* * *

Lying stiffly beside Charlotte in their makeshift bed, Adrienne's thoughts were not so very unlike Lucien's, though she did not wish herself a peasant. Nay, she wished Lucien were a lord. It was cruel for the Fates to tease her with a man like him, who was everything she wanted and nothing her grandfather would want for her, because Lucien was neither noble nor landed. And only a man with bloodlines or property would be allowed to wed her.

Chapter 5

"Lie down, John. You're dead!" young Hugh declared.

"I am not!"

"You are! I plunged my sword into your heart," the heir to Fortengall informed his younger brother, brandishing a toy weapon for emphasis.

"You didn't. I've barely a flesh wound."

"I saw Hugh run you though," the other carrot-topped twin declared soberly.

John's face reddened, as if he were holding his breath, and his plump cheeks puffed out. "Jamie, you're a traitor!" he wailed in a high-pitched, childish screech.

From the opposite end of Fortengall's great hall, Lady Lucinda's eldest son rose from the stool on which he'd been seated, trying to converse with Peter and Raven. Slowly he turned toward the squabbling youngsters and, noting that none of the three was even aware of him, he bellowed at the top of his lungs: "Enough! Quiet down, you raucous pups, or I'll run all of you through with *my* sword!'' Threateningly, he placed his hand on the hilt of his sheathed weapon just as his little half-brothers turned to gaze at him.

The youngest twin boys' chins began to quiver, tears streaming down their cheeks. But Hugh's chin went up a notch. Indignantly, he informed Lucien, '' 'Tisn't fair! I killed him, Lucien, I did. But the little—''

''Hugh!''

All six of Lady Lucinda's sons turned at the sound of that voice each knew so well. But the Earl of Fortengall, fairly filling up the entire archway with his massive frame, kept his eyes on his own eldest, his heir.

''John and James are younger than you, lad. You must go easy on them 'til they match you in size, at least. And you're not to call either of them names,'' he added, knowing full well that had been Hugh's intention. '' 'Tis a beautiful, warm day beyond, so get yourselves outside. Now!'' he commanded, and without further urging, all three boys skittered past their sire to scramble out the door.

''Children,'' Lord Ian snorted, shaking his head as he pushed his heavy chair into the small circle that Lucien, Raven, and Peter had made of their stools. '' 'Tis glad I am I did not have to go through the raising of you three. Though I would have been younger then, had I fathered you.'' He eased himself into the chair and accepted a mug of beer from Peter. ''Those three,'' he said, nodding his head in the direction the children had fled, ''are aging me faster than your mother could.''

Raven grinned. ''What would you do without our fair mother?''

''I know not,'' he replied candidly. ''I dare not think of it.''

''And your sons?'' Peter put in. ''Methinks you'll miss them sorely when they go off to foster. And that shan't be long now. Three years left for the twins, and one less for Hugh.''

The earl threw back his head and laughed heartily. ''You don't think Lucinda will allow them far from her skirts, do you? Nay, she intends each of you to nurture one of them. John with you at Stoneweather,'' he told Peter. ''James with you at Stonelee,'' he told Raven. ''And Hugh, of course, with his eldest brother at Eynsham.'' With that pronouncement, Lord Ian settled his gaze on Lucien.

''Then I'd best get on with making it mine,'' he said grimly, aware his tone bespoke his foul mood. But Lucien had reasons: He'd had but a few scant minutes sleep the night before, he'd found his only clean pair of leggings with a hole in them, his favored falcon was molting unhealthily, and those squabbling tykes had near driven him to distraction the whole afternoon long.

''I assume you three were making plans,'' the earl surmised. ''Have you come to some decision?''

Lucien frowned. ''What decision is there but to storm the damned keep?''

''I should have thought you'd consider smaller details.''

''What details?''

''Details that could better help you defeat your enemy,'' the earl explained. ''Knowing Osric as you do, surely there are some.''

''Know him?'' Lucien snapped. ''I know him not, nor do I wish to. Yet I intend to defeat him in the same manner he defeated my father—and me—by attacking with so large a force, he's no choice but to surrender.''

''Or die trying to resist,'' Raven added.

''Aye, or die trying,'' Lucien agreed.

The earl shook his fair head slowly. ''That's not the way to go about it, my lads. Use your heads while they're still attached to your shoulders. They are far mightier weapons than the swords you carry.''

Lucien felt his face flush hotly. He should have delayed this discussion 'til another time. This day he was tired, distracted, and his patience worn thin. Yet he tried to stifle his irritation as he addressed his stepfather in a slow, even voice.

"Lord Ian, I wish you'd not speak in riddles. What is it you're implying?"

"I'm saying you must know your enemy."

"Again I say I've no wish to know him!" The younger knight pushed up off his stool and strode toward the cold hearth. "All I wish to know *about* him is that he is dead, or at least gone from my home so that I may return to rule there as its lord."

"But what," the earl said to Lucien's back, "if you gather your forces and attack, and Osric defeats you? 'Tis no easy thing to capture a keep. The odds are against the attacking forces if those inside are well prepared. Behind stone walls there is safety, as there is for a turtle within its shell. While the lord and his people are warm, dry, and secure, those outside the bailey walls are subjected to the weather as well as to boredom, when they are not being tortured with a torrent of arrows and baths of boiling oil."

"Perhaps in a keep such as this castle," Lucien agreed, still staring at the blackened fire pit. "But you've stables that are more well-built than Eynsham. Osric cannot keep me out any better than my sire, Gundulf, could keep *him* out."

"Has nothing changed in the years since Osric declared himself Lord of Eynsham?"

"What?" Lucien spun on his heel and glared at the earl.

"I simply inquired if there had been changes made, most particularly to the keep. Has the moat been widened?"

Lucien blinked. His stepfather's words were like a spray of water dashed upon his face. "There—there is no moat."

"At least," Peter remarked thoughtfully, "there was no moat when Eynsham belonged to Gundulf."

Lord Ian shrugged. "If there was but one bailey, are there now two? Have the walls been heightened or reinforced?"

"I—I don't know." The admission was forced through Lucien's clenched teeth like tough meat through a grinder.

Yet the earl continued calmly with his questions. "What of Osric's men? You three have told me of the surprising number of knights Osric led when he attacked your father. How many has he now?"

"Well, surely he hasn't the number he had when he attacked the keep those many years ago," Raven surmised. "His knights were mercenaries—had to be. Now his holdings must be guarded by the usual number of men-at-arms."

"What is the usual number?" Lord Ian cocked an eyebrow that had been skewered and divided in two by the tip of some foe's sword.

The twins glanced at each other before settling their gaze on Lucien, who felt the prick of their stares and the weight of the silence that ensued.

"I've no idea what the usual number of men-at-arms might be," he admitted. "No more than I know if there is a moat or the walls have been built up."

"Sit down, Lucien," Lord Ian urged casually. " 'Tis no disgrace to be ignorant of a place you've not seen in half a dozen years."

"But I should know!" Lucien insisted angrily, his sword hand clenched in a fist as he took his seat again. "I'm a knight, for sweet Jesu's sake. As you said, milord, a knight should know his enemy."

"Many's the soldier who's battled an unknown enemy. Surely you all have done so in the past. Often 'tis a knight's skill with a sword, a mace, or an ax that makes him the victor over another."

"Aye." Lucien nodded his head dejectedly. "So it will be for most who follow me to Eynsham. But as their commander, I should know both the man and the place we're up against so I do not lead my men to their deaths in sure defeat."

"Lucien," Raven said, reaching out to put a kindly hand on his brother's shoulder, "don't berate yourself. Like you, Peter and I have held in our minds the image of Eynsham Keep as we knew it. Never did it occur to us, either, that Osric might have fortified it, or that he retains a heavy guard." He glanced at his twin, who nodded. "Besides, you've spent all these past years in service here and to the king. When might you have ridden to Eynsham to observe?"

"God's teeth!" Lucien grumbled, rising again to pace heavily toward the hearth and back again. "I've been such a dolt. All this time my concern has been for money with which I could pay my men. I fear I forgot the importance of detail." Lucien returned to stop before the earl's chair. "My thanks, Lord Ian, for pointing out my failings."

"Don't whip yourself bloody over it, Lucien," the older man said kindly as he smiled up at his wife's eldest son. "I've been a lord and a knight and a commander of men far longer than you. 'Tis only right I pass along the bit of wisdom I learned along the way." He reached up and fingered the long, dark scar that ran the length of his face, from eyebrow to beard. "Besides, it is easy to lose sight of logic in the heat of passion . . ."

The earl continued speaking, but his words evoked a sudden, unbidden image of Addy in Lucien's mind. It riled him that she could intrude upon his thoughts, especially now, when he needed a clear head. Yet as he envisioned her, naked and wanton, her shimmering hair pooling beneath her in a dark green bed of moss and ferns, he acknowledged she had been like a pebble in his shoe the whole day long. She rubbed him sore so that he could not ignore her.

"Lucien?"

Hearing Peter speak his name, Lucien was pulled from the depths of his private thoughts. "I'm sorry," he apologized to his brother. "I was thinking."

"Oh? What were you thinking?"

"That I must travel to Eynsham to learn more of Osric and to discover the condition of the keep."

"We'll go with you," Peter and Raven volunteered, speaking as one.

"No. I shall go alone."

"You can't!" the brothers protested.

"I can." Lucien looked from one to the other of the dark-haired, dark-eyed brothers. "It will be much easier and less conspicuous if I travel alone rather than the three of us riding together. I've no wish, after all, to arouse Osric's suspicions."

"He's right," Lord Ian told the twins. But, looking up at Lucien, he advised, "You'd best make some pretense of being other than what you are."

"Disguise yourself as a monk," Raven suggested.

Lucien pulled a face. "I think not! I'm hardly monkish."

That declaration beckoned another image of Addy, which he forcibly dispelled with a shake of his head.

"Besides," he continued, "I should probably have to ride a damned ass if I posed as a monk. Since I intend to make the trip quickly, I shall go as an outlaw and ride my own mount."

"Merlin? That great destrier?" Peter scoffed. "Not as an outlaw, dear brother. Besides, if anyone suspects you to be an outlaw, be they peasant or sheriff they'll hang you, or worse."

"What then?" Lucien demanded impatiently. "I don't intend to wear a wimple and pose as a lady!"

"Why not ride the roads as the king's man?" Lord Ian suggested. "It would be no disguise, really, for you've served Henry much of these last six years. Do you still have some proof that you are a knight in King Henry's service?"

"Yes, I do." Lucien nodded. "I have a passport signed by his own hand, for when he sent me across the Channel from Clarendon to Gisors. I have it still in my valuables casket."

"Good."

"But it says—"

"Lucien, what the document says matters not. If you need it to prove yourself to anyone, simply wave it beneath the beggar's nose. Mayhap the man shan't be able to read. If he can, all he need see is Henry's signature and seal. "Now," the earl continued, "when do you intend to depart?"

"Immediately."

"But, Lucien' " Peter pointed out, "the sun is hanging low in the sky. Why don't you wait 'til the morn—"

Peter's suggestion went unheard except by his twin and their stepfather. Lucien was already striding out of the great hall, heading for the stairs.

He was riding out of the castle gate, heading for Eynsham, just as a nearly full moon began rising in the dusky, twilight sky.

Adrienne and Charlotte lay side by side in the bed of Wills's wagon. They were deep in the king's forest, alongside a road that was more grass than dirt, and which no one would ever have marked on a map. Their campfire, beside which the peddler slept, was small and cast only a dim, flickering light. Were it not for the full moon and stars, Adrienne thought she could not have been able to see her hand in front of her face.

She was examining the little pewter angel, holding it close to better inspect it. But she already knew every line, every curve, and her thoughts wandered elsewhere.

"I don't much like it in the forest," Charlotte whispered suddenly. "Outlaws roam the forests."

"Lottie, nothing happened to us on the way to Fortengall. Nothing shall happen to us on our way home. Remember, we're dressed like poor peasants."

"But Wills has a casket of coins, now."

"Only we know that. Don't worry, Lottie."

Charlotte rolled from her back to her side, facing Adrienne. "Are you well?" she asked in concern. "You've been awfully quiet this whole long day."

Her first instinct was to deny it. But Adrienne decided instead to speak of what plagued her mind. Raising herself on one elbow, she peered down into Charlotte's face. "Lottie," she whispered, "might you consider defying Grandfather and returning to the convent?"

Charlotte's eyes went so wide the whites gleamed as bright as the moon. "Never!" she gasped, pressing a hand to her chest. "How can you suggest such a thing? Defy him! He is our guardian and I—we—must obey him."

"We rather defied and disobeyed him by going to Fortengall Fair."

"It was your idea! Besides, he did not actually say nay, that we could not go, because we never asked him."

"You never asked him if you could return to the monastery at Ford," Adrienne pointed out.

With a sigh, Charlotte sat up. "Addy, you know he intends for us to wed. He made that clear at the first. There was no need for me to ask him if I might return to the convent of holy sisters. I knew full well he'd deny me."

"But he's naught to us, Lottie," Adrienne said as she,

too, sat up. Distractedly, she began picking straw from her hair. "He was our stepfather Edward's sire. We had not even met him during the years Edward was married to our mother. Why must we now obey him in all things?"

"Why? Because the old lord took us in when we had no one, nothing. Do you not recall, Adrienne, how it was when we returned to the manse at Brent? Both Mother and Edward dead, their bodies burned, not buried. Even the house was gone."

Adrienne closed her eyes. She remembered it well. It had not been that long ago, the end of last year's summer. She had left her parents—her mother, Anne, her stepfather, Edward—in good spirits and good health, to visit Charlotte at the convent where her sister had been studying the past three years. Adrienne had been away but a few sennights when the message came: Edward had died of the pox.

Both the girls left Ford hurriedly, riding hard, with only Brother Tristan as escort. But when they arrived at the farm that had been their home, they found nothing but a charred ruin. Their old servants tearfully explained that even before Edward died, Anne had taken sick with the pox. She followed her husband quickly, and those in the village, fearing the deadly and disfiguring disease would spread to them, burned their corpses, the manse, and nearly all the family's possessions.

Adrienne's eyes teared at the memory of the acrid smell that had clung to every blackened timber.

"Brother Tristan took us to Edward's father," Charlotte recalled. "And he took us in willingly, providing for us ever since."

"He needn't have," Adrienne said petulantly. "You could have returned to the convent at Ford and taken your vows as you'd hoped to."

"And what of you?" Charlotte demanded. "Addy, the

last thing you want is to marry the Church. If Grandfather had not taken us in, made us his wards and his heirs, what would have become of you?"

Black lashes closed over blue eyes as Adrienne pursed her lips. What Charlotte said was true. She'd have had no life were it not for Edward's father. What could she have done? Gone to London town and worked the streets as a whore? Married some crofter, to toil beside him on the land? She'd been born a lady, and though her home had been a great farm instead of a great demesne, and her house a manse, not a castle keep, she had not been raised to live a hard, mean life like some serf. Adrienne knew she'd have had no future were it not for the kindness and generosity of the man who urged them to call him their grandfather.

Stubbornly, though, she rubbed her thumb over the small, metal angel she clutched in her hand, and told Charlotte, "Only if you dare to return to the sisters and take your vows will you ever be truly happy. And if you did so, Grandfather would understand, I'm sure. He is not unkind, and with you away at Ford, he'd no longer have to provide for you."

"But—"

"Hear me out," Adrienne begged, grabbing Charlotte's arm. "I could accompany you. I, too, could join the convent and take my holy vows. Then neither of us would be a burden to our guardian any longer, and we would both be happy."

"Both be happy?" Charlotte repeated, frowning at Adrienne with an expression of total disbelief. "You would never be happy married to Christ! Always you have dreamed of a husband and children."

"No more." Adrienne shook her head emphatically. "I've changed my mind."

For a long moment, the elder sister studied the younger

in the dim glow of the small fire and the large moon. " 'Tis he, isn't it? Lucien.''

"Lottie, nay."

"It is! That stranger, that reeve, has caught your fancy, and now you've convinced yourself you'll be satisfied with no other as your husband." Charlotte huffed. "Lady Adrienne, you are being a foolish girl. Sweet Mother Mary, you spoke but a few words to him. He's nothing to you! Yet because of him, you would not only disappoint our guardian, you'd make yourself miserable for all your life by becoming a nun?" She stared hard at her sister. "Addy, what ails you?"

"Nothing." Adrienne did not sound as adamant as she'd intended to, but she continued, "I have just decided I've no wish to wed some stranger Grandfather chooses for me. Given the choice, I'd much rather make my way with you back to Ford. There we could take our vows and remain together always, and husbands would ne'er be a consideration."

For a long minute, Charlotte said nothing. Adrienne hoped she might be considering her suggestion. But when she finally spoke, it was clear she had not.

"It's no longer possible, Addy. Not now," she said. "Had we returned there immediately after discovering Mother had died with Edward, then, aye, we could have done it. But not now. Now we've lived nearly a year on the old lord's charity. And besides, he has made us his wards and his heirs. His lands are our dowerlands. We are beholden to him, Addy. And he needs us to wed so that finally, someday, he'll have male heirs to inherit his fee."

"But we are not truly his family!" Adrienne protested. "Any sons we might bear would be no more his blood than we are. We should not be obliged to marry at his decree."

"You're wrong, Adrienne." Charlotte shook her head

before lying down again and tugging the scratchy blanket they shared up over her chest. "Grandfather made us his family, and now we must fulfill our obligations to him."

Adrienne scowled, but she argued no more with her sister. As she, too, snuggled back down into the straw, she muttered, "I wish I were truly a peasant. Then I could do as I wished, marry whomever I chose."

"Nay, you do not," Charlotte countered softly. "If you truly felt that way, you'd never have accepted Grandfather's invitation to live in his keep. You'd have stayed in the village of Brent or made your way to London. But you did neither."

Charlotte, Adrienne knew, always spoke the truth. So though her sister dispensed a bitter potion, Adrienne felt compelled to swallow it. Still, she felt trapped and helpless, and the little angel Lucien had bought and given to her failed to soothe.

Sleep was hard in coming and so fitful, Adrienne disbelieved she had so much as dozed. Yet suddenly, she was startled from her vagary of dreams by a shrill scream that raised the downy hair on her arms. She shot upright in the peddler's wagon, her eyes wide in alarm.

What Adrienne saw stilled her heart for an instant. Charlotte, arms and legs thrashing, was being dragged out the back end of the dray. Her captor seemed a ruffian with a sneer on his face and a dirk in his hand, which he held close to Charlotte's throat.

In the moment it took for her heart to resume its frantic beating, Adrienne saw Charlotte disappear and another fearsome stranger lunge into the wagon. This one grabbed Adrienne, and she found that, like her sister, she was helpless against his greater strength. Futilely, she screamed, bucked, and flailed. But with two sinewy arms snaked about her, the dirt-encrusted, broken-nailed fingers of one hand on her breast, the other foul-smelling digits clamped over her mouth, she was yanked unceremoniously from the wagon bed and hauled to the ground below.

"Be still!" the villain holding Charlotte shouted. "Or we'll cut yer bloody tongues out."

Immediately the girls, who stood facing each other, their backs to their captors, fell silent. But only for a moment.

"What have you done to Wills?" Adrienne soon demanded. "Where is he?"

"You mean the old peddler? 'E's where you left 'im, wench—sprawled upon the ground."

The girls' eyes darted toward the place they'd last seen Wills. They discovered him still near the little cookfire, but no longer was he stretched out, snoring, atop a bed of tattered blankets. The tinsmith lay silent as the dead, blood glistening wetly on his balding pate.

Chapter 6

Lucien had made good time. The moon shone like a torch, lighting his way, and alone on his massive warhorse he had done more than half a day's ride under cover of darkness. He had ridden hard for good reason—the exercise eased his exhaustion, and the closer he came to his destination, the less he was distracted by thoughts of a peasant girl he would never see again.

Suddenly, a feminine scream cut through the night sounds like the screech of a carrion bird. Lucien reined Merlin in, and the beast's ears went back as Lucien scanned the forest with narrowed eyes. A second voice joined the first in a series of ear-splitting shrieks, just as he glimpsed a tiny dot of light ahead—a flicker of light that Lucien surmised might be a campfire.

The knight's blood raced. His primal instincts flared, urging a hasty, noisy charge forward to discover what lay ahead. But years of training overruled his more barbaric and incautious impulses. Kneeing his steed, Lucien rode on slowly, as silently as he could manage.

"You've killed him!" Adrienne shouted, glaring at the cur who held Charlotte against his chest. "You whelp of a dog! Why? Why would you slay a helpless old man?"

Silently, the outlaw toed the tinker's money casket, which lay on its side near his foot.

"For coin?" Adrienne cried in disbelief. "You killed for coin?"

"Many's been killed for less, bitch," the man spat. "An' I suggest you be 'oldin' yer tongue, slut, or I be carryin' out my threat first on this one 'ere."

Still clutching Charlotte securely about the waist, he pressed the flat of his knife blade against the curve of her chin.

Adrienne stiffened as she grasped the seriousness of his threat to her sister. Complying with his demand, she fell silent again.

"What now, Robbie?" the ragged thief holding Adrienne asked his companion. "We got the ol' man's pennies."

"An' we also got us two fine lookin' wenches." Robbie leered at Adrienne, his stained teeth appearing bright in contrast to his darkly bristled cheeks. As he eyed the fair-haired beauty his cohort held secure, he began fondling the bosom of the dark-haired damsel he held close to his chest. When he began kneading the soft mound of flesh, Charlotte's eyelids drooped and her shoulders sagged, portending an inevitable swoon.

"Stop!" Adrienne begged.

"Stop?" Robbie snapped, his dark eyes widening as he glared hostilely at Adrienne. "You dare to order me about?

You be no better than I, bitch. Besides, I warned you, 'old yer tongue or I cut this girl's out.''

"Nay!" she cried again, a desperate plea as she watched the man plunge his grimy fingers into Charlotte's mouth.

"Jesu, but I canna' stand the noise these two make," he declared, releasing Charlotte except for her tongue, which he held between his thumb and his finger.

Adrienne's gaze remained on her sister, who stood awkwardly, bent at the waist. Though all that pinned her to the spot was the villain's filthy fingers pinching her extended tongue, Charlotte made no effort to pull away, to flee. Dismally, Adrienne realized Charlotte was not even thinking of escape. She was paralyzed with fear.

"Milord, allow me speak," she begged, addressing the beggarly thief as if he were a high and mighty noble.

It caught Robbie's attention. "Aye?" he asked curiously, arching one black brow as his gaze flicked from Charlotte to Adrienne.

"I beg you not harm her. The girl is—simple. She rarely speaks at all. Even you know I'm the one who's made the most racket. But I vow I shall keep my peace if you refrain from harming her."

"Simple?" Robbie turned to better consider his captive. "But comely, eh? All the better she doesn't speak. I don't need 'er flapping this 'ole." To demonstrate, he yanked on Charlotte's tongue, making her gag as her mouth gaped open further. "Nay, the only 'ole I've an interest in is 'idden."

With a flourish, the creature grabbed the hems of both Charlotte's tunics, hoisting them high. Not only were her pale legs exposed to the others, but also the thatch of dark hair at the apex of her thighs.

Adrienne's eyes sought Charlotte's. Vainly, she tried to share her own strength with her sister. But Charlotte did not respond. Her dark eyes were glazed.

"Let her be!" Adrienne demanded, twisting and pulling in an effort to wrench herself free from the man who held her. "I told you, she's simple. In her mind, she's no older than a child."

"I don't give a bloody good damn!" the one called Robbie declared, though he did drop Charlotte's skirts again. "She's no child in face or figure."

"If you want a woman, use me," Adrienne offered impulsively.

"There be two of us," the one behind her declared, as if she were unaware of that fact.

"You can both have at me."

"Why should we, when we can each 'ave one of our own?" Adrienne's personal captor said into her ear. His breath, even on her neck, was foul enough to make her grimace.

"Because she's a virgin, and considering the fright you've given her, she'll do naught but lie beneath you like a log. But I'm no stranger to men," she hurried on breathlessly, seeing that Robbie looked intrigued by her offer, "and I'll pleasure you both 'til your eyes roll back in your heads."

" 'Til our eyes roll back, eh?" he repeated. "I'd like t'know 'ow you'd go about that, wouldn't you, Gilly?"

"Aye, Robbie. I surely would."

Robbie abruptly released Charlotte. He shoved her away with the flick of his wrist. Charlotte stumbled back and fell on her bottom, where she sat for a moment, a stunned, stricken expression on her face. Then she dropped her head and her thick, dark hair, hanging loose, covered her face like a veil. It hid her eyes and shielded her vision.

Relieved that she had diverted the men's attention from her sister, Adrienne exhaled a pent-up breath. But she inhaled another breath of terror when Robbie took a predatory step toward her, and Gilly leaned into her from behind. Together, they forced her between them.

" 'Old 'er tight, Gilly."

Adrienne felt the arm binding her waist flex. She saw Robbie's dirk gleam dully in the firelight as he approached. He was nearly on top of her now.

Closing her eyes to block out his hellish visage, Adrienne could not ignore his cohort's arm as it squeezed hard beneath her ribs, nearly cutting off her wind. Neither could she be deaf to the sound of rending cloth as her bliaut and undertunic were ripped from her neck to her waist. Nor could she disregard the cold steel of Robbie's blade pressed hard against her throat.

At first Lucien thought he had only imagined the cloak of shimmering hair when he saw the girl snared between two grinning miscreants. When he knew it was truly Addy, not a trick of light or mind, it took a moment for him to regain his sense of calculated detachment. Indeed, it took a strong will to remain some seconds longer, hidden by the trees, as he assessed the situation.

There were only the two outlaws. But both men were armed, each with a quiver of arrows on his back, bows slung over their shoulders, and knives in their hands. Lucien had only his sword and his dagger. He knew that if he charged in swiftly, he could take one out. Yet the other might have time to shoot or otherwise harm Addy. So Lucien forced himself to wait in hiding a few more agonizing moments, until the time arrived for him to descend like an avenging angel. He would slay both the beggarly bastards, and rescue the damsel before she suffered more indignities at their hands.

Addy stood stoically as Lucien watched the man before her rip her tunics down the front, wrenching the fabric away. The one behind her yanked the garments off her arms, yet still she stood unwavering, wearing nothing but her linen smock, which thinly covered her breasts and only scantily covered her bottom. When the men cackled and chortled in glee, licking their lips in lewd anticipation, Lucien felt a twisted knot of pain in his chest that he had felt but once before—the moment he knew Eynsham Keep was lost.

"What a comely piece you be," the man brandishing the knife declared. He leaned forward, pressing his mouth on Addy's.

Lucien watched as she remained rigid, enduring the wretched kiss. He winced when the man, still forcing his mouth hard on hers, dipped his hand into the edge of her shift and began pawing her breast.

"Sweet Jesu!" the villain declared when he raised his head for a breath. "Look what we got ourselves, Gilly!"

The ruffian seized Adrienne by the shoulders and spun her around so that his friend, Gilly, could better see their prize.

She looked impossibly small and fragile in the thin moonlight that filtered through the leaf-laden branches above. Where last night, to Lucien's eyes alone, she had appeared ripe and womanly, now, displayed to prying eyes she'd not invited to look upon her, Addy seemed waiflike and preciously young.

He ground his teeth. He pulled on Merlin's reins, and the horse raised its huge head in anticipation. The moment approached, though it had not yet arrived. Impatiently, the knight and his steed waited.

"God's blood, but she's a beauty!" the man, Gilly, declared. "Let me 'ave a go at 'er first," he begged, already shedding his quiver and bow.

"I be in charge 'ere," the other announced. As if he assumed that that declaration were enough to make Gilly wait his turn, the other outlaw threw off his own weapons, except for his dirk, whose blade he bit between his teeth.

"Bloody 'ell you are!" Gilly argued, hoisting his tattered tunic to reveal his bare legs and a throbbing erection. " 'Sides, I grabbed this one from the wagon. The one you took be sittin' yonder like as if some witch cast a spell on 'er."

The outlaw, Robbie, unable to speak with his knife between his lips, scowled and growled at his companion before pushing Adrienne to the ground. When she sprawled on her back, he scrambled over her, pinning her there with one hand to her shoulder while he fumbled at the ties on his leggings with the other.

" 'Old on there!" Gilly whined.

And Lucien charged. As Merlin ate up the distance between their hiding place and the trio near the fire, Lucien threw his dagger at the back of the man crouched above Addy. It met its mark surely. With a gasp, the outlaw's dirk dropped from his teeth and he threw back his head, arching his neck. When he crumpled sideways and rolled off his victim, the other cur turned with a cry toward the sound of pounding hoofbeats. Staring in horror at the rampaging steed bearing down on him, he brandished his own knife helplessly. It was too small and too far from the mounted knight to do any harm.

Lucien's knife had barely left his hand when he drew his sword and swung it hard. He scored the second man's neck from ear to ear, sending blood spurting in a crimson arc before his victim fell, limp as a straw doll, to the ground.

All went silent, all went still. Lucien reined Merlin in and sat, for a moment, staring at Adrienne. She, in turn, looked up at him and then at the corpses nearby.

She broke the silence with a scream. The shrill, piercing sound curdled Lucien's blood. Instantly, he leapt off his destrier. He grabbed Adrienne and held her tightly to him.

"Addy, 'tis I. Lucien. Lucien!"

Again and again he repeated his name, trying to penetrate the terror that kept her shrieking. At last her screams subsided, softening into fitful sobs as she clung to him, her face buried in his hauberk.

"You're shaking. Let me cover you." He unclasped the pin at his shoulder and wrapped his own cloak about her trembling form.

Adrienne's terror shattered, and the shards fell away. Encompassed by strong, familiar, comforting arms, the fear she had bit back in her efforts to spare Charlotte crescendoed and faded. As her breath hitched convulsively in her throat a final time, she managed to ask, "Wills? Did you see him? Is he truly dead?"

Hearing his name, the peddler roused enough to sit. Both Adrienne and Lucien turned at the sound of his labored movements. "Nay, lass," he declared, touching his bleeding scalp tentatively with the palm of his hand. "They got me right good, but they didna' do me in.

"My money," he said sharply, scanning the campsite. "Did they get me casket?"

Adrienne shook her head, wiping away tears with the back of one hand and motioning to the little brassbound wooden box with the other.

Lucien strode toward Robbie's inert body, rolling it over with his foot. He picked up the casket the corpse had fallen upon and handed it to Wills, who smiled contentedly at having it back again.

"Addy."

Charlotte's voice was weak, but she stumbled up and over to her sister just as Adrienne began scrambling toward her. The sisters embraced as though they had not seen each other for long years.

"Oh, Addy, I'm sorry," Charlotte wept brokenly. "I failed you."

"You didn't. What could you have done against such men as those?"

"But I did not—I did not even try to help you. 'Twas as if I were a pillar of salt—"

"Lottie, don't. It's over. Neither of us was harmed. Both of us were saved." Adrienne set her sister away. "Could you get me some different clothes?" she asked. Glancing down at Lucien's cloak she added, "Those I was wearing are . . . ruined."

"Yes. I'll get them." Apparently eager to do something helpful, Charlotte hurried to the wagon.

But when she returned with a bundle in her arms and fell into step beside Adrienne, who had already turned away from the little camp to head deeper into the trees, Lucien said softly, "I think not, mistress."

The sisters drew up short, whirling around to face their knightly rescuer. "I have to dress," Adrienne told him. "You understand."

"I understand you shan't leave my sight again, 'til you've reached your destination safely."

"But—"

It was Charlotte who dared attempt a protest, and Lucien's gaze settled on her.

"Do not delude yourself that these two"—he motioned to the dead thieves with a jerk of his chin—"were all there were. They might have been traveling in a band, the others still nearby."

Charlotte gasped while Adrienne nodded. It was foolishness, Adrienne knew, to plead for privacy when Lucien had seen her in less than her shift during the long night they had spent together. Besides, it warmed her heart to see no lust in his gaze, only tender concern.

"Do not be overly frightened," she whispered to Charlotte. " 'Tis best to be cautious. Besides, we can be discreet."

With a nod of her own, Charlotte placed herself between Adrienne and the knight. Slipping his cloak from her sister's shoulders, she used it to shield Adrienne's near nakedness from the man whose eyes did not once leave Adrienne's face.

It was no longer dark, though not yet day—that time when the sky fades from black to indigo as the sun hides the moon and the stars.

Lucien studied Adrienne. Her hair was wild and tangled and feral, tumbling over her shoulders and disappearing behind her back; her black-lashed blue eyes glimmered like jewels reflecting candlelight. She seemed even more beautiful tonight than she had been at Fortengall. He would readily slay an army and dragons, too, to keep her safe.

Suddenly, surprisingly, Lucien knew he must have her— not only for another tumble in the grass, but forever. He smiled, pleased with the fortuitous turn of events that could make it possible. Surely she realized now that he was no serf but an avowed knight, sworn champion of women, children, the downtrodden, and both the king and the queen. Surely, too, she knew him as the kind of man even she would consider becoming mistress to.

Adrienne was fully garbed now, and when Charlotte stepped aside she found herself considering Lucien as though seeing him for the first time. In her terror, she had recognized only his arms, his voice, his scent. But now she took in his appearance. He wore a shirt of mail and fine, loden chausses that matched the soft wool cloak he'd wrapped her in and which, still, she held in her arms. Though it rested in its scabbard now, she recalled seeing the flash of his sword's blue steel blade, which Lucien had wielded so skillfully. All were part of a costume that went with the rounded helmet Adrienne spied hanging on his horse's saddle—a chestnut horse with a glossy black mane and tail, a horse so massive and powerful, so fearsome and well trained, it could belong to only one sort of man.

"Lucien," she said.

"Lucien?" Charlotte repeated, her brow furrowed with a frown as she glanced again at their heroic rescuer.

Adrienne ignored her. "Lucien, you are neither serf nor servant. You're a knight."

"Aye." He nodded slowly. "In service to King Henry and Queen Eleanor."

They might have said more to each other then, but both were distracted by a soft thud as Charlotte's body crumpled to the ground. She had, belatedly, fainted.

Chapter 7

Though Charlotte roused to Adrienne's gentle shaking, Lucien scooped the girl up in his arms and settled her in the back of the dray. Wills was already harnessing his mules when Lucien reached for Adrienne, intending to lift her into the wagon as well.

"I would speak with you," she whispered urgently as his hands clasped her waist.

"Nay. Day is nearly upon us, and I was not trying to frighten you unduly when I suggested there might be other outlaws about. 'Twould be best if we set off quickly now."

"But, Lucien—"

"How far to your destination?" he interrupted, swinging her up into the wagon despite her protestations.

"In this conveyance, one full day's ride and part of another. Surely, though, you were headed elsewhere when you happened upon us."

"But riding due west, as you are." Lucien smiled and

chucked Adrienne's chin. "Do not fear you delay me from my business. Even if you did, sweetling, I would still insist on seeing you safely home."

Adrienne felt a guilty pang; Lucien calling her "sweetling" stung like a dash of salt on an open wound.

"What is it?" he demanded, his frown mirroring her own. "Are you still distraught over what nearly happened here? Addy," he urged when her mouth opened wordlessly, "speak to me. You may tell me anything."

"Can I?"

"Aye, of course. Always."

"Well. I—I—"

It was no use. Adrienne could not bring herself to tell him the truth. Not yet. Not so abruptly.

Blinking, she broke eye contact with Lucien before sweeping the ground with her gaze. "The angel Wills made, the one you gave me. I fear I've lost it."

"Is that all?" Lucien laughed easily. " 'Twas nothing but a trinket. You, however," he added seriously, reaching out to cup Adrienne's chin in his hand, "are the real angel. And glad I am not to have lost *you*."

He was too good, Adrienne thought miserably. Such a chivalrous knight—so brave, so strong, so caring—even toward a girl he hardly knew, whom he thought a lowly peasant.

"I'd best help the old man get his wares back into the dray, else we'll be here 'til noonday," he announced suddenly. Lucien preceded his remark with a throat-clearing cough and ended it by stepping back from the wagon.

A bit disappointed at losing his company but greatly relieved to be leaving this dreadful place, Adrienne helped arrange the barrels Lucien tossed up into the wagon bed to allow herself and Charlotte room for the ride. When he mounted his destrier and took the lead on the road, she knelt in the straw, clinging to the wagon's slatted side.

Thus, she was the last one to view the little campsite they were gladly leaving. The grass was tamped, the fire a ruin of ashes. And the outlaws' corpses remained, to rot or feed the wolves that lived in the forest.

Charlotte dozed fitfully as they bounced slowly along the bumpy, overgrown road, and Adrienne, holding her sister's head in her lap, gently stroked her brow.

She should have told him. She should have told Lucien she was a lady nobly born. Of course, he had not told her he was a knight, not once during the time they'd spent together at the fair. But knights without arms or armor rarely looked knightly—he'd not meant to deceive her by the simple clothes he'd worn.

But she had meant to deceive him. All because she'd feared the loss of his attentions if he knew she was his better. Sweet Mother Mary! Was it too late to confess? Would Lucien be angry that she had thought him a mere serf, mayhap a servant in some lord's house, nothing better? Would he think her coarse and common as the clothes she wore because, in spite of her gentle birth, she'd cavorted with a stranger she believed to be less than her equal?

"Aye, he will," Adrienne muttered miserably, looking down upon her sister's furrowed brow. " 'Twould have been better had he not rescued me. Then he'd never know of my deceit."

A new thought struck her: If she and Charlotte feigned that they lived in the village of Evandale, Lucien would still be none the wiser. He would go his own way—on that quest of his, no doubt—and she would go hers, to wed the lord her guardian chose for her. Aye, that was it! But . . .

Knowing that Lucien was Sir Lucien, knight of the realm,

in service to King Henry, made it more difficult for Adrienne to accept the faceless man her grandfather would urge her to wed. Much more difficult than it would have been before she went to Fortengall Fair; even more difficult than it would have been had she still believed her lover was a man of humble birth. God's wounds!

Impulsively, Adrienne turned and craned her neck, stealing a glimpse of Lucien on his steed. At that same instant, Lucien turned around in his saddle, his eyes going to hers as if she'd called to him. With a solemn nod, he touched two fingers to his helmet in a silent gesture of recognition. Blushing furiously, Adrienne righted herself to face the back of the dray.

There had to be a way out of this, a way through it. If Lucien cared enough to risk his life while believing her a simple village wench, surely he would still care for her if he learned she was a lady.

"He is a knight, I am a lady," she whispered beneath her breath. "No matter what our garb on the day we met, clothes should be no reason for us to be separated. Should they?"

Suddenly, Adrienne knew. The answers came to her swiftly, like autumn leaves flying in the wind. Happily, she squeezed closed her eyes and silently thanked the Fates she'd so recently been cursing. They had not been teasing or tormenting her, as she'd first surmised. Nay, they were clever, those unseen forces who dictated the course of people's lives. They'd brought her and Lucien together in a way she would never have dreamed, and then revealed— to herself, at least—the promise of a future they might share.

Riding Merlin, Lucien was lost in his own thoughts. As Adrienne contemplated him, so too he contemplated her. He should have been thinking of Eynsham Keep and Osric, his enemy, who called himself Lord of Eynsham. But the wench kept distracting him, so Lucien gave himself up to thoughts of her. God knew he had enough time to dally with idle musings—his pace had become excruciating slow since he'd taken it upon himself to see Addy and her companions to their destination.

Something pulled at him. Turning around, he discovered the focus of his thoughts, the object of his desire, gazing at him thoughtfully. He raised his hand, giving her a small gesture he hoped conveyed much. He also hoped she was as eager to lie with him again as he was eager to lie with her.

Facing forward once more, Lucien tried to ignore the heaviness that had suddenly swelled between his legs. As he considered the seemingly endless forest that loomed before them, that surrounded them, that seemed even to follow behind them, he prayed to the angels that night would fall early. If it did not, and he was prevented from taking his ease with Addy before his cod exploded, he would simply be compelled to march into the forest alone and kill a boar. 'Twould be no problem, he thought wryly, that he had no boar spear among his possessions. He could stick the beast with his rigid cock!

It seemed Lucien's prayers had been answered, for at midday clouds rolled in. Some hours later, the sky darkened ominously, not with impending nightfall but with the threat of rain.

"We should stop for the night," he announced. He had turned Merlin around and now rode beside the peddler's wagon. "Storm clouds are gathering. It will be dark soon, and 'twould be better to prepare for rain rather than get caught in it."

"Y'er right, m'lord," Wills agreed. "Find us a wider spot on the road, and I'll rein the beasties in."

"I'll catch us some game for supper," Lucien offered.

"And Lottie and I will gather wood for a fire," Adrienne volunteered.

"Nay, a fire?" Charlotte protested. "Do you think that safe, Sir Lucien?"

He considered the pale, doe-eyed damsel but a moment before smiling reassuringly. "Of course it is safe, mistress. We'll need it for warmth and to cook our food, as well as to keep any animals from straying too near. If you are worried about outlaws attacking again, I beg you, do not. I'll protect you. Besides, the foul weather will send any roaming bands of villains scurrying for cover just as surely as it does us."

"There, do you see?" Though Adrienne spoke to her sister, she smiled at Lucien. "We've naught to fear with a knightly escort."

"A knightly escort," Charlotte repeated as she clutched the side of the dray and looked up at Lucien. " 'Tis hard for me to believe you are truly a knight of the realm, milord. I thought you little more than a high-ranking servant or, mayhap, a bowman, when I first spied you at the fair. To learn you are as gently—"

"We mustn't detain Sir Lucien now, Lottie," Adrienne interrupted. "He must find a suitable place for us to wait out the night and the rain. Is that not so?"

"Aye."

With relief, she watched Lucien ride off at a brisk pace. In her musings, it had not occurred to Adrienne that Charlotte, in all innocence, might reveal their true identities. Now her desire to confess the fact that had so far eluded Lucien's attention was spurred anew by a sense of urgency.

Yet settling in for the night was no quick task, despite their lack of accoutrements. The spot Lucien deemed suitable lay some distance farther up the rutted, rocky road. Time dragged by interminably until Wills finally halted his creaky wagon at the place where Lucien awaited them.

Next there was the staking of tent poles and the hanging of Wills' threadbare cloth over them to form a shelter. They had to stretch old hides over the wagon bed to keep its contents dry. Lucien went off, taking with him a confiscated bow and some arrows to hunt game for their meal, while the sisters gathered wood so that the peddler could start a fire.

Impatient, Adrienne still tread cautiously, one ear ever trained on the others' conversations. Fortunately Charlotte, never one for careless banter, seemed of no mind for polite chatter this eve. She went about her tasks silently. And when the hares Lucien caught for their supper were cooked to a golden turn, she sat by herself eating little, pondering much, and saying naught at all.

Lucien sat beside Adrienne as they shared a short, rotting tree trunk as a makeshift bench. The knight ate as though it had been a long while since he'd last supped. With a sensual relish that seemed almost sinful, he licked clean the bones of his meal and the fingers of each hand. Adrienne, however, found that, like her sister, she had no great appetite. Yet she did not find the right opportunity to speak in confidence with Lucien, despite her watchfulness.

Not until Charlotte, at last, spoke up.

"How shall we sleep tonight?" she asked as she tossed the remains of her meal into the flames.

Glancing sidelong at Lucien, Adrienne found him studying her appraisingly, one eyebrow raised in a rather suggestive manner. She nearly blushed, but she managed to volunteer, "I would suppose beneath the canopy."

Wills agreed. "Aye, that's right. Plenty o' room for all of us under the tent. You canna' go crawling into the dray—you'd perish fer lack of air under those skins. Besides, the fire 'ere will 'elp abate the dampness."

"Very well." Charlotte stood and went to the wagon,

poking her head beneath the hides as she rummaged in the straw for blankets.

"Lucien," Adrienne whispered, turning to him.

"I would have a few moments alone with you, Addy," he returned, coming to his feet and taking her hand so that she rose with him. "A walk, mayhap? Not too far, I vow."

"Aye," she agreed, relieved. She hoped she did not sound overeager.

"Addy?" Charlotte had returned to the shelter, her arms full of the frayed, itchy rags that passed as blankets. "Shall I make up your pallet, too?"

"Yes, please, Lottie. But"—She stole a glance at the man beside her—"I shan't be coming to bed straight away. Lucien and I are inclined to take a short walk."

"What! Now? Addy, you shouldn't."

"We won't go far," Lucien promised. "And I'll have my sword with me."

Charlotte blushed and lowered her chin. "It's not that, milord. I've no concern for my own safety. 'Tis only that it's nigh on full dark now, and surely 'twill begin to rain at any moment."

"As I just promised Addy, we shan't go far. Before you hear half a score of raindrops hissing in the fire, we'll be with you under the canopy."

Charlotte brought up her head with an audible sigh. "Very well. Goodnight, then."

Wills cocked his balding head, his eyes darting between the couple on his one side and the solitary girl on his other. "Come on, lass," he said to Charlotte. "While I fix me own pallet, I'll tell you o' the time I saw our good king's grandsire, old King 'Enry hisself."

"You didn't! Did you, truly?"

"Wills doesna' tell tales. Not to beautiful young women like yerself."

As the peddler kept on talking, he glanced over his shoulder at Adrienne and Lucien, sparing them a wink.

Adrienne blushed guiltily, but when she glanced up at Lucien, she found him grinning at the peddler as though they shared a secret.

Taking her hand in his, he led her deeper into the trees. "Come," he whispered as he sought their privacy. "Before the rain does indeed start falling."

Adrienne raised her face to the sooty skies. She could feel the moisture hanging heavily about them and, like a child, stuck out her tongue to taste the air.

Beside her, Lucien groaned. "Don't do that. Not unless you intend to pleasure me with that wicked tongue of yours."

They remained so near the little camp that the firelight filtered through the trees. Yet Lucien turned to Adrienne and pulled her into his arms. His mouth descended on hers, and he captured her moist, pink tongue between his even teeth.

"Lucien!" Adrienne gasped when he finally released her lips.

"Addy."

His hands roamed boldly over her body, as though he needed to reassure himself that she was real. "I cannot tell you how I felt when I realized 'twas you those two, vile creatures intended to ravish."

"Nor can I tell you how I felt when I realized you had slain them both to save me."

So neither tried. Instead they tumbled onto the forest floor of fallen leaves, moss, and pine straw. Adrienne did not know how or when Lucien stripped her of her tunics. But with keen appreciation, she watched him remove his own clothes while he crouched above her.

Her champion, her savior, was indeed the most exquisite man on earth, Adrienne decided dreamily. His shoulders were broad, his biceps bulging; his smooth warm chest was hard with muscle, as were his taut thighs and belly. And from the coppery pelt at his groin rose a fine, proud member that declared his desire for her. Though her own body itched with driving, carnal need, she knew she could be quite content simply gazing at Sir Lucien, noble knight of King Henry's.

But Lucien could not be so content. When he looked down at Adrienne as he knelt between her knees, she appeared to him a mythical siren who stoked the fire of his passions to unbearable heat. With limpid eyes and languid smile, she drew him to her and he went willingly, eagerly. Threading his fingers through Adrienne's, Lucien's mouth pressed hard on hers. He needed no guidance, but slipped inside her hidden cleft and rode her hard until the inferno inside him exploded with a burst of colors in his mind and a spurt of seed from his loins.

When her lover entered her, the lady felt whole. Bucking and straining against him, she seemed driven to take all of him into her, as though fashioning a cocoon of her own flesh to wrap about him. In her efforts to encompass him, to cleave to him, to meld with him, she, too, scaled the heights of her own passion and teetered at the precipice until he bade her fall with him, fall safely encircled by his arms.

Again, as before, they nestled in the woodland nest they had made with their bodies, their garments. In the misty shadows of this early evening, Adrienne's surroundings appeared fuzzy and wavering, as though she lived in a dream. If it were a dream, she wished never to wake.

"We must stop trysting like this."

"What!"

" 'Twas merely a jest," Lucien assured Adrienne with a smile. "But I should like the opportunity to make love with you in a soft, dry bed. These twigs and stones can be distracting." As he spoke, he reached beneath his bare backside and retrieved both a twig and stone, which he tossed aside.

But Lucien's humor was lost on Adrienne. Her heart had quickened at his confessed desire to make love with her in a bed. His words betrayed a desire for a future together.

"There's something I must tell you," she said quickly.

Lucien, enfolding her in his arms, squeezed Adrienne gently. "There is something I wish to say to you, also."

"Let me speak first," she begged, turning her head to look up into his face. "Lucien, when first we met, both Lottie and I presumed you to be a humble man of common birth."

"I know. She said as much. Does it disturb you, to find I'm something more?" He gazed at her intently as he awaited her answer.

"Nay, Lucien, it does not. Glad I am you are a knight well trained who spared me from those vilest of men. Nay, it disturbs me not at all."

"Good. That pleases me."

"Does it? Then—then this should please you more: I am no peasant, Lucien. In truth, I am a lady born."

She made her admission on a rush of breath. Now she inhaled deeply, her eyes trained on his handsome profile.

"A lady?"

"Aye. My Christian name is Adrienne, and my sister is called Charlotte."

"Lady Adrienne. Lady Charlotte." Lucien spoke evenly, but she detected an edge to his voice that made her uneasy. "Why?" he asked. "Why did you present yourself as other than what you are?"

"Lucien," said Adrienne, turning in his embrace to more fully face him, "Lottie and I slipped away from home while our grandfather was gone away. Traveling with Wills to the fair, we thought it better not to be dressed as noblewomen. And when I met you, I thought— Well, I didn't realize you were a knight, so I presumed you would not like me much if you knew I was gently born. Thus . . .'' She shrugged and waited.

Lucien stayed silent. He could feel a muscle in his jaw twitching and supposed Addy—Lady Adrienne—could see it. But he could not make it cease, and he did not care. He had just lost her forever! No chance of making love with her in a soft, dry bed now. She was a damned *lady*, a lady who would have expectations of a knight who deigned to court her. Hell, a knight who dared *seduce* her and take her maidenhead! God's wounds, but Lucien wished she were really and truly no more than a serf, born to humble parents who worked the land. Then he might have persuaded her to become his mistress after all. But now . . .

"Lucien?'' His name on her lips was a question, timid and wary.

"Aye,'' he returned gruffly as he released her, stood, and gathered up his braies and leggings.

"Are you angry?''

"Nay.''

"But—'' Adrienne came to her knees and grabbed the hem of his tunic as Lucien shrugged it on. '' 'Tis no real difference, is there, if we both be lowborn or high? We are the same people we were upon meeting, only now we can claim to be something more than mere peasants.''

"We are not the same.'' Lucien set his jaw, and his green eyes narrowed. "You have your life with your sister and your grandsire, and I have my quest, which I have vowed to my God and myself to see through to the end. We should never have met, we should never have—'' With a broad gesture, he intimated much and implied very little.

Adrienne had been so hopeful. Now Lucien had dashed

those hopes. Too late she realized she should not have discarded her initial fears so easily.

"You think me a slut, don't you?" she demanded accusingly. "As a lady born, you believe I should not have given myself to a man I'm not wed to, a common man at that. No matter that the common man was you!"

"Nay! Never would I think such a thing," Lucien insisted.

"Then why are you so cold? How can you ignore what's gone between us? How can you turn your back on me?"

Her voice was a hiss, kept low by the need for quiet, strained by uncried tears. Lucien heard her pain, and he wished he could comfort her. But touching her was a risk he could not take.

"Adrienne, it's naught to do with you," he insisted softly. "It's to do with me."

"That is a lie!" Scrambling up, wrapping her bliaut around her body to cover her nakedness, she glared at him angrily. "I was good enough for you when I was Addy, a peasant, but I'm not good enough for you as Lady Adrienne. Why not, Lucien? Tell me! Why not?"

"God's blood, Addy!" He leaned toward her so abruptly, so ominously, she had to step away. "Do you think I make a habit of deflowering innocent damsels of noble birth? Jesu!"

Angrily he spun around, giving her his back as he buckled his belt and secured his sword. The rain fell now in definable droplets. He ran his fingers through his wet hair before turning to face Adrienne again. "If you were widowed or even still wed, and I'd known the true circumstances of your heritage, 'twould not have mattered. I've had many lords' widows and wives. Or," he continued, advancing on her, "if you were truly what I believed you were, a comely, saucy village wench intent on having her first man, 'twould have been of no consequence, either.

But you were a virgin, you are still a lady, and I—" Lucien paused, unwilling but determined to say the rest. "I have ruined you."

Adrienne flinched as if he had struck her. She understood now. When he thought her a humble woman of no importance, he'd been happy to debauch her. But now that he knew her to be a lady, deserving of his honor and respect, he had no intention of doing right by her. He would not consider wooing her, let alone asking for her hand. Nay, he regretted having taken her innocence, the bastard!

She was livid. When she'd learned he was a knight, the likes of which her guardian might approve, she'd fantasized a future with Lucien. But when he'd learned she was a lady, Lucien could not run away fast enough. Not only had he broken her heart, he'd sorely wounded Adrienne's pride.

Drawing a deep breath and righting her naked shoulders, down which streamed rivulets of rain, she declared, "I have always known I was a lady, Lucien. I was also well aware of my virgin state while I still remained a chaste damsel. Though I readily succumbed to *your advances,*" she explained pointedly, a sneer in her voice, "I never once entertained the notion of taking you to husband."

It was no lie, so her words rang true. Adrienne had *not* considered wedding him when she was first bedding him. Thus Lucien had to have heard the conviction in her voice. She felt considerable satisfaction, though not nearly as much as she felt with her next pronouncement.

"Don't worry that you have ruined me, sir. I am made of better stuff than you suppose. 'Twould take being pricked by more than your weapon to see me laid low."

Lucien's face burned; Adrienne had scored a direct hit. Yet he did not react, though he ground his teeth as he motioned to the clothes she hugged to her body.

"Get dressed. The rain's begun to fall in earnest. We need to take shelter with the others, and I need a good night's sleep. I've been awake for days."

Obedient only because she was shivering, Adrienne pulled one tunic on over the other, belted them both, and then searched for her shoes in the damp underbrush.

"Where is it you live?" Lucien addressed her bent back.

"That is no real concern of yours, my lord," she replied crisply as she straightened, leaned one hand against a nearby tree, and pulled a felt shoe onto her dainty foot. " 'Tis not even another full day's ride in the dray to my grandfather's keep. I'm sure Wills, Lottie, and I can make it there without your protection. You, sir, are free to go about your business."

"You did not get even this far without my protection. Besides, I promised to see you safely home, and I shall."

"I repeat, it is not necessary." Adrienne yanked on her second shoe.

"Where is it you live?" Lucien demanded again, taking a long stride toward her and reaching out to grab her elbow.

Wrenching her arm free, she scowled up at him. For a moment, Adrienne considered keeping silent. Yet she knew the effort would be in vain. Were Lucien as determined as he appeared to be, he could simply continue to ride along with their small party until they all reached her destination. Besides, she had to consider Charlotte. Charlotte, who still trembled in the aftermath of their ordeal, would want the gallant knight, Sir Lucien, as their escort and protector, rather than to proceed in the company of old Wills.

"This road will get us home," she informed him grudgingly. "Another full day, possibly less with the mules and the wagon, and we'll be at Eynsham Keep."

Lucien did not flinch, he did not even blink. "Eynsham Keep?" he repeated.

"Aye, that's the name of it. Our grandfather is Lord Osric of Eynsham."

Chapter 8

Lucien rode some distance ahead of the peddler's wagon, his face a stony, craggy mask. Despite his exhaustion, he'd slept little the night before, and his sleep had been thin, punctuated by distressful dreams.

Jesu! he thought sullenly. If there truly were Fates who moved humankind about as though they were game pieces on a board, then they were surely having a hearty laugh at his expense just now. How could it be? How could Addy, the comely but uncomplicated village girl he'd thought she was when he first met her, prove to be both a lady born and his most hated foe's close kin? Christ, 'twould be easy to believe that not only their first encounter at Fortengall but her subsequent peril on the road had all been contrived for his benefit. Yet Addy—Lady Adrienne—had been naked in the rain when she'd begun volunteering details of her life. A conniving, conspiring bitch would never have told him the truth while so exposed and vulnerable. She'd never have confessed the truth at all! Or would she? Even now, as Addy trailed him in the wagon, did she lead him into a trap set by Osric?

His eyes were aching with fatigue and Lucien covered them with a gloved hand. Confused and angry, he fought the urge to suspect the damsel he'd so recently hoped to make his mistress. Yet he knew he should be cautious. Could it be random chance that the saucy young gentlewoman who appeared to be a mere peasant at his stepfather's fair—and who succumbed so eagerly to his advances—just happened to be Osric's granddaughter?

Lucien sighed, dropped his hand, and found himself coming around a bend in the road. Thatch roofed huts and cottages lay directly ahead, flanking the rocky, rutted cart path. He drew a sharp breath. It had been as many years since he'd seen this village—Eynsham's village—as it had been since he'd last seen the keep itself. He wondered if a complement of Osric's guards loitered there, in Evandale, leisurely awaiting his arrival. Or if, perhaps, one lone marksman with crossbow and bolt was even now targeting him.

Suddenly it didn't matter. If he, Lucien, son of Gundulf and rightful ruler of this little hamlet, were doomed to be cut down, he'd meet his death sitting tall on his destrier, not skulking, disguised, in nighttime shadows.

Impulsively, Lucien squeezed Merlin's sides with his hard legs and galloped fast into Evandale. Scattering dust and villagers 'til he reined in his mount, he ignored the gawking townsfolk as his eyes scoured every rooftop and shadowed doorway for some knight intent on slaying him. But Lucien saw no one save the poor serfs who dwelt in this town. Relaxing in his saddle, he took stock.

Evandale was small by any measure. The lord of Eynsham and his men-at-arms protected the villagers. In return, the crofters shared the task of working the lord's portion of the common fields; they used the lord's mill to grind their grain; and they paid a portion of their harvests for that privilege. Evandale had always been a poor, mean community, as the soil the villeins toiled was hard and rocky, difficult to farm. The livestock were always skinny, their ribs showing through their hides, and, as Lucien recalled now, the people themselves were perpetually dirty and garbed in threadbare rags. Though his mother had done what she could for them—and that was little enough, as Gundulf had often forbade Lucinda to fulfill her role as healer to the peasants—babes frequently died only days out of the womb, while adults limped on mishealed bones or succumbed readily to any vagary of illness.

Lucien's memories of Evandale were not particularly pleasant, especially as they now came to mind. So, sitting astride Merlin in the middle of the rough road, he found himself bemused.

The village had grown. Far more cottages lined the stony path, and the crofts leading from behind the dwellings to the common fields were littered with pecking chickens, rooting pigs, and cud-chewing cows. At the far end of the road from which he'd approached stood a church. So fast had he ridden past it, Lucien had hardly noticed it. But now he saw that it was no ordinary church of daub and wattle or even timbers. No, this one had been constructed of stone so that, despite its diminutive size, it would last centuries beyond the life of the local lord who'd had it built.

Lucien's inadvertent thought of Eynsham's impostor lord brought his eyes to the hill that lay but a brief ride ahead. He had purposely kept his glance from straying there. But now, like Moses daring to look upon the burning bush, Lucien bit back his dread and gazed full at it. There stood his home, *his* home, Eynsham Keep.

God's tears, but it had changed, just as Lord Ian had

suggested it might. No moat had been dug, but it was obvious that the bailey walls had been heightened. And, as they did at Fortengall Castle, guards visibly patrolled Eynsham's parapets. At either side of the gate, a rectangular tower had been erected. In the open window of each stood a knight, both of whom, he knew, had trained their eyes on him.

"Milord! Milord!"

The children in the crowd surrounding him had lost their awe of Lucien while he'd sat so passively, so quietly, on his steed. Now they grinned and giggled, a few daring to reach out and pat Merlin's flanks. Returning their smiles, Lucien tossed figs to them, which they grasped in their grubby fingers and ate greedily, the sticky fruit staining their teeth.

Adrienne came upon this scene as the wagon in which she stood finally bounced into Evandale. It struck her that Lucien looked at home in such a setting, a kindly lord passing out treats to his people's children. She wondered if he had a keep or a castle coming to him sometime, somewhere; a barony, perhaps, where he would indeed reign as its generous land-lord. She felt a small sting as she realized that she would never know.

Wills brought the cart to a stop a short distance behind Lucien's horse. Charlotte was on her knees, clinging to the wagon's wooden sides. "Addy, we're home!" she exclaimed softly, her relief evident in the smiles she gave the children who gathered around the dray.

"Aye. And safe, despite our misadventure. Also, we've returned far ahead of Grandfather, so we'll not be reprimanded for sneaking off."

From the corner of her eye, Adrienne glimpsed Lucien turning around and riding back toward the wagon. Steeling herself for his farewell, she spoke first. "You may be on your way now, sir, for you've fulfilled your promise to see us safely home. Up yonder," she pointed, "is our grand-father's keep."

Lucien blinked slowly. His clenched jaw twitched. "Osric of Eynsham's keep, is it?"

"Aye."

For a very long moment, neither Adrienne nor Lucien moved. She watched him watch her, though she suspected he saw her not at all but rather looked through her. A chill of foreboding swept over Adrienne, and she would have spoken then except that Charlotte asked before she could, "Sir Lucien, are you well?"

He blinked and glanced her way. But before Lucien could utter a word, all of them, including Wills and the villagers, were distracted by the thunder of heavy hooves. They looked toward the keep to see one of Osric's men galloping down the motte toward the town.

The knight, in full armor, reined in his mount, causing the horse to turn and prance before settling down. "Sir Hubert of Lord Osric's guard," he declared himself to Lucien before he spied Adrienne and Charlotte in the peddler's wagon. "Holy Mother of Jesu! My ladies, your grandsire has been beside himself with worry. Where have you been?"

"He's here?" Charlotte squeaked.

"Aye, Lady Charlotte. Lord Osric returned two nights past, and he has been frantic over your welfare. He sent out a search party, but they returned midmorning without you and without word. Where did you go?"

"I am sure," Lucien replied in the sisters' stead, "the ladies can explain their recent whereabouts directly to their grandsire."

The Eynsham knight eyed him speculatively. "And who might you be?"

"Sir Lucien, a friend of Lady Adrienne's and Lady Char-lotte's."

Hubert's expression was grim as he studied the alien knight. Yet when his gaze slid to the two young women in the dray, he smiled at them kindly. "Methinks it might be best if your escort, Sir Lucien, accompanied you both to the keep when you make your explanations."

"Grandfather is that angry?" Charlotte asked apprehensively.

"Not so very angry," he assured her gently. "I would say he's been distraught."

"M'ladies—" Wills spoke up finally, turning around to face his passengers. "You don't need me t' be explaining t' Lord Osric what you've been about, do ye? I must be on me way, y' know."

"We know," Adrienne assured him as she grabbed her bundle of belongings and jumped, unassisted, to the ground. While reaching up to help Charlotte from the conveyance, she continued, "You go on about your business, Wills. And thank you for taking us along."

"My pleasure." The old man nodded and pulled an imaginary forelock. Casting Sir Hubert a quick frown before raising his eyebrows at Sir Lucien in a commiserating look, Wills whipped his mules' rumps, forcing the beasts to lurch forward and his small wagon to roll on through the village at its fastest speed.

For a moment, the two young women stood between the destriers and their riders. Again, Adrienne spoke up.

"I know you have urgent business as well, Lu—Sir Lucien. Lottie and I would not delay you by having you accompany us as far as the keep."

He observed the sisters from beneath lowered lids. Charlotte frowned fretfully, her slender fingers flexing and unflexing. But Adrienne appeared composed, her shoulders back, her head high. She was being brave again.

"I have a little time," he admitted. "Give me your hand; I'll carry you up to the keep."

Adrienne hesitated only a moment. When she put her hand into Lucien's, she felt a spark burn her palm that raced up her arm to her heart. She found it unnerving that his slightest touch could so affect her; without success, she tried to keep herself away from him when she settled into the saddle in front of him. But that proved impossible. Lucien took up all of his saddle, forcing her to nestle her backside into his spread thighs where she could feel the bulge of his manhood, trying, in turn, to nestle into the cleft of her buttocks. Nor had she any recourse but to lean her back against his chest as his arm anchored her to him.

Hubert lifted Charlotte onto his own mount, and the four of them rode out of the village and up the well-used hillside trail that led to Eynsham's gate. Though Lucien could have led the way blinded, he decorously followed Hubert and Charlotte. He saw much that appeared heart-rendingly familiar, but his reaction was tempered by the distraction of Adrienne sitting in his lap. With every step Merlin took, her bottom bounced delightfully against his sex, tempting it to swell. And with every step her unfettered breasts jiggled against his arm. These minutes, he thought, had to be the most tortuous he had ever known.

Yet he could not have abandoned Adrienne outside Eynsham's walls as he had earlier been inclined to do. He had to protect her from Osric's wicked temper; he owed the lady that much for having stolen her virginity. More importantly, Lucien could not dismiss the opportunity to slip within the bailey, perhaps into the keep itself. The invitation was too fortuitous to ignore in favor of risky disguises and stealth. To ride boldly into that place Osric held as his own—ah! What a humiliation it would be for the old lord when later he realized what Lucien had done.

The portcullis was closed. Hubert waved to the guards in their towers and shouted, " 'Tis the ladies Adrienne and Charlotte! Raise the gate!"

The familiar sound of chains and creaking metal brought the spike-toothed gate up high enough for the riders to go beneath. The knights kicked their steeds, and the horses trotted briskly into the yard.

Inside the bailey, every muscle in Lucien's body tightened. Seeing the place where he had been born hit him harder than seeing the village. Part of him felt as if he'd ridden back in time; yet another part of him felt like a stranger from another land.

Eynsham Keep remained the same, yet it was different.

The outbuildings looked familiar, though certainly these had been rebuilt since Osric's victorious raid. There were the armory and the granary and the stables. But there was a barracks now to house the large number of Eynsham's permanent guard. And the people—their faces looked different. Not only because children had grown to adulthood and taken their parents' places as servants to their lord, but because . . . they looked well and content. Under Gundulf's rule, everyone save the lord and his family were beggarly, and even the family went wanting. Men had walked with stooped shoulders, the women cowed. Now Lucien saw smiles and heard friendly banter all around. It had been the same in Evandale, Lucien realized with a start.

Seated across his thighs, Adrienne felt Lucien's body go tense, as though he sensed an imminent attack. She did not understand, but she had no time to puzzle it out, for she had her own concerns. There, on the top step at the front portal of the cylindrical stone structure called Eynsham Keep, stood its lord, her guardian.

"Grandfather!" she shouted hastily, sliding down off Merlin as if the beast's saddle had caught fire. "We are home!"

She ran to the old lord, smiling, hoping that Charlotte was close on her heels. "I'm sorry if we worried you, my lord. But we thought to be back before you returned from your journey.''

Charlotte had followed Adrienne, though she remained silent. Both Hubert and Lucien dismounted, striding forward until they stood behind the sisters.

Lucien observed his old foe, surprised to discover him a man heavy with years, his balding pate wreathed by a fluff of unkempt gray hair. If he'd worn a coarse tunic and sandals instead of leather boots and hunting attire, Osric would have looked like a typical friar, Lucien thought. Even as he was, he did not seem the evil, fearsome knight who had crushed both Gundulf and Lucien himself beneath his heel.

"If we gave you a fright, we are heartily sorry." Adrienne continued, rushing on breathlessly, as though she feared what her grandfather might say if she paused long enough for him to speak. "Lottie and I did not think you'd be returning to Eynsham for another sennight yet.''

"You presumed you'd be back before me, eh?" Osric asked, cocking one bushy eyebrow as he considered his fair-haired granddaughter.

"We did not mean to deceive you," Charlotte put in quickly. "Nor should we have gone! We nearly—"

Adrienne swiftly silenced her sister by stepping firmly on Charlotte's toes.

As Charlotte choked back her words and jumped aside, Lucien stifled a smile. He admired Adrienne's subtle move; she'd been discreet, her quick footwork hidden by the hem of her gown. But she had been effective.

"We shouldn't have gone without your permission, Grandfather," Adrienne elaborated, picking up where Charlotte had abruptly left off. "But you were not here, and the opportunity presented itself.''

"The opportunity to do what?" Osric demanded sternly.

"To go to the fair.''

"What fair?"

"Ah . . ." She hesitated, apparently debating between telling a truth she did not care to confess and a falsehood she'd not yet invented.

"Carrington." Lucien spoke for her.

Adrienne spun around. Her eyes showed surprise that he had named a hamlet much nearer to Eynsham than Fortengall. He hoped she understood he'd spoken for her and Charlotte's benefit, as he could not elaborate. He was busy bracing himself for exposure.

Osric's speculative gaze moved from the maid to the man. Yet before he could comment, another lord, a younger man of middle years, stepped through the doorway behind Osric.

"Wilfred!" he exclaimed, his attention diverted as he caught sight of the newcomer from the corner of his eye. "I'd thought you were elsewhere inside the keep."

"Charlotte, Adrienne," he continued, turning to his wards, "meet my old comrade, Wilfred of Houghton. He has been searching for you as avidly as I, and that was not the purpose of his visit here." Again, his gaze returned to Lucien. "I do not believe we have met, my lord."

"I am Sir Lucien. Currently bound in service to his royal majesty, King Henry."

"You are!" Osric's eyebrows shot up. "Well, come in, my lord, and take your ease in my humble abode. We must discuss this matter of my granddaughters' disappearance, and 'tis best we not continue in the yard."

Lucien had no time to reconsider as he followed the man who'd killed his father into his stolen keep. Adrienne's hand rested gently on his arm as they entered together, while behind them Hubert escorted Charlotte inside the great hall.

A wave of homesickness rolled over Lucien; it was so acute he felt nearly nauseous. He'd have given a great deal, then, for a long moment of privacy within these walls to observe and reflect. But circumstances forced him to pay heed to the conversation of those around him, and it surprised Lucien to realize that only Osric was making polite chatter. The others stayed silent, while Wilfred of Houghton appeared downright sullen.

Cautiously, Lucien eased into a chair before the hearth while Hubert excused himself and left the hall. When all who remained were seated, each accepted a cup offered by Eynsham's steward. Stretching out his long legs and crossing them at the ankle in a posture of ease, Lucien allowed himself to relax. He, Gundulf's heir, was no more visible than an evening breeze to the people in this hall, and Osric no more suspicious of him than a penitent of his priest. He had nothing, at that moment, to fear.

But Adrienne and her sister did; it was apparent by their pale, pinched expressions. Lucien glanced at each of them, sitting on either side of his chair, and determined to do what he could to see them spared the harshness of their grandsire's wrath.

"Sir Lucien, I fear I've not yet introduced myself," the lord of the keep admitted. "I am called Osric of Eynsham."

"I'm aware of that, my lord." The gall tasted bitter in Lucien's mouth as he forced himself to address his host, his foe, with such respect.

"Though I should like to know more of you and how you are acquainted with my granddaughters, that must wait until we've resolved the issue at hand." Osric's pale blue eyes flicked between the two young women. "Adrienne, tell me now why you and your sister went off to the spring fair at Carrington. You told no one, and all my servants knew was that you disappeared the morn an old peddler left Evandale." He shook his head in disapproval, a frown deepening the creases in his brow when neither volunteered an explanation. "One of you, please—account for your actions!"

The old man's gaze settled on Charlotte, but Adrienne responded to his exasperated demand. " 'Twas a whim, Grandfather!" she said. "We thought to enjoy the fair and be back at Eynsham before you even knew we were gone. We'd no wish to concern you."

"Concern me!" He gripped the arms of his chair and leaned forward. "Adrienne, if you'd no wish to concern me, you'd at least have taken one of Eynsham's knights as escort and protector!"

"I performed that task, my lord." Lucien, too, leaned forward so that he sat nearly nose to nose with Osric. The gesture put him between Adrienne and her grandfather. "I happened upon the ladies Charlotte and Adrienne when they were barely out of sight of Evandale. As I was on my way to Carrington as well, I offered to serve as their escort."

"But were you not a stranger, sir?"

"Nay." Lucien sat back as Adrienne spoke up, straightening her spine.

"Of course Sir Lucien is no stranger," she insisted, risking a sidelong glance at Charlotte. "He fostered near Brent, our childhood home, and we have known him since we were very young."

"This is true?" Osric asked, easing his own girth more comfortably back into his high, carved chair.

Not one of the three responded quickly. Both Lucien and Charlotte looked at Adrienne, he with appreciation for her quick wit, she as though her sister had grown horns.

Finally Lucien looked back at Osric. "Aye," he confirmed, "it is true. I fostered with . . ."

"Lord Sedgewick," Adrienne put in, taking up her cue as if they had rehearsed this scene. "He has a fine estate very near Brent. Doesn't he, Lottie?"

Charlotte blinked as though awakening from a deep sleep. Yet she nodded her head in affirmation.

"Aye?" Osric, one caterpillar of an eyebrow raised speculatively, glanced from Charlotte to Lucien to Adrienne. "But you did not leave Eynsham with him. 'Twas only by chance you met him on the road. What if you had met with outlaws instead? They'd not have protected you! They'd have robbed you or—or worse!"

"Oh!"

Charlotte's exclamation was a sigh that bordered on a moan. Paling visibly, she shrank against the backrest of her chair.

Jumping up, Adrienne hurried to her and whispered in her ear, "Lottie, please say naught, nor counter anything Lucien or I might say. 'Tis best we not confess how far we really traveled nor how close to death we really came."

Adrienne straightened and returned to her chair. "I fear Charlotte is lightheaded, Grandfather. We must confess to being famished. It has been a long while since we had our last meal."

"Charlotte, you should have spoken up immediately," Osric chided. Clapping his hands, he quickly summoned servants who hurried to comply with his request for platters of victuals so that everyone, his granddaughters most especially, might be replenished.

Returning his attention to Adrienne, he regarded her thoughtfully. "I still require an explanation. What were you thinking when you rode off with a peddler? You had no armed knight to protect your purse or your purity when you set off. Why would you do such a thing?"

Lucien watched Adrienne patiently, awaiting her response. Realizing none was forthcoming, he lowered his eyes to where their hands rested side by side on the respective arms of their chairs. Moving his, he surreptitiously brushed hers.

"The damsels were foolhardy, my lord," he announced bluntly, meeting Osric's gaze. "I doubt either would deny it. But as Carrington is so nearby, they thought there would be little chance anything untoward might happen during their brief journey."

"Aye." Adrienne nodded in agreement and heaped more details on the pile of growing lies. "That is precisely what we told him when he came upon us. Sir Lucien, however, being much wiser than we, made it clear our assumptions were wrong. Therefore, he accompanied us and saw us safely home again."

The old lord exhaled loudly. "I owe you my thanks, then, sir, for seeing to the welfare of my granddaughters. I'd not expected such reckless behavior from young ladies of their age."

" 'Twill never happen again, Grandfather," Charlotte promised.

"Indeed it shan't," Wilfred agreed.

The girls and Lucien looked at Osric's guest, surprised by his curt comment. He went on: "Your guardian deems the time ripe to see you two wed. I'm inclined to agree, for with husbands to, ah, shall we say . . . protect you, you'll neither be free enough to put yourselves in danger again."

Both Adrienne and Charlotte stared unblinkingly at Wilfred of Houghton; then they turned to share a look with each other. Lucien, meanwhile, considered the stranger speculatively. His comment had been presumptuous and audacious; Lucien wondered what the man's business might be here at Eynsham with Osric. He wondered, too, if Wilfred would prove a fly in his own porridge.

"Is your business on the king's behalf urgent, sir?" Osric inquired, abruptly changing the subject. "Or have you time to accept my hospitality? I should very much like to have you as my guest, if you're willing. 'Tis little enough I can do to repay you."

Lucien was taken aback, Wilfred's presence no longer of any real interest, either keen or casual. In his wildest dreams, Lucien had not imagined his enemy blithely offering him hospitality. Mayhap those Fates of Addy's were not just pranksters after all.

Curling his lips in a smug smile, Lucien replied, "Oh, I should be delighted to stay a while, my lord. Nothing would please me more than to accept your invitation."

Chapter 9

Minutes later, Lucien's self-satisfied mood was swept away on wings of rage. Stepping into the chamber provided him, he slammed headlong into his past. In childhood, this very room had been his; seeing it now, again forced something inside him to give way. As if his rigid control had been a dam that burst, a torrent of emotions erupted, frothing with fury.

" 'I am called Osric of Eynsham,' " Lucien mimicked, repeating the old lord's words as he kicked at the narrow bed. " 'Called', indeed," he growled. "For you are not the rightful lord of Eynsham, nor shall you ever be!"

He sat down heavily, the mattress sagging under his weight. With a disdainful eye, he considered the room's well-worn accoutrements and snorted, "You may have raised your bailey walls and hired scores of mercenaries to serve as your home guard, Osric. But you must be poor as a church mouse if you still retain Gundulf's decrepit furnishings!

"You pathetic fool," he growled, though his voice had dropped to a whisper he alone might hear. "You invited me inside your keep where, by morning, I can easily slit your throat ear to ear."

Lucien fell backward and cradled his head in his locked fingers. A grim smile curled his lips, but only for a moment. It took no longer for him to admit he could never commit such a cowardly act. Besides, to murder Osric in his bed would be too kind—he would never gift his foe with so quick an end. He recalled too well the fear, the frustration, the valiant yet vain effort to hold Eynsham when Osric attacked it. Far more than wanting the bastard dead and gone, he wanted his old enemy to know the agony of those fears and that same aching sense of loss that came with defeat.

With his eyes closed, Lucien recalled in vivid detail the day Osric had attacked his home.

It had been a spring day, mellow, sweet and cloudless. None would have expected an attack had Osric's army not been spied upon the road riding toward Eynsham.

"Osric." It was a name then rarely spoken in Gundulf's keep, the name of a cousin who believed he'd been cheated out of Eynsham when their grandsire, Ranulf, declared that upon his death, the fee should come to Gundulf. Though the story had been told so often that Lucien and his brothers recognized the name, it had been a score and five years since their father had been declared Lord of Eynsham, and in that time naught had been heard of Osric.

Yet there he was, suddenly, riding down from the north country toward the demesne of his kin. There had been just time enough to spirit Lucinda away from the keep before the attack. But there had been little Gundulf could do to ensure the defense of his home. Because both the demesne and the village were so poor, and because he did not involve himself in politics, Gundulf retained only a small number of knights and men-at-arms. Despite his own sword arm and those of his newly knighted sons, then, he was doomed to be outnumbered and overpowered.

Still lying upon the creaky bed, Lucien threw an arm over his closed eyes in an attempt to shut out the recollections that rushed in on him. But he could not. The sights, sounds, and smells that had assaulted him since entering Eynsham's bailey had given new color to faded memories. He recalled standing on the parapets, amazed by the seemingly endless column of knights rushing toward his home. They'd ridden fast and hard, attesting to Osric's plans to attack swiftly rather than lay siege.

And attack swiftly they did. With grappling hooks, ropes, and ladders, the men scaled the walls like nimble spiders. For every knight Eynsham's archers felled with well-aimed arrows, it seemed two knights replaced them. Like locusts they invaded the yard, mercilessly slaying every living creature between them and the keep itself. Once inside the keep, they fought sword to sword and staff to staff with those who defended it and set to flame everything that would burn, from the rushes on the floor to the hangings on the walls.

Lucien's throat went dry as he remembered the stench of the heavy smoke that scorched his lungs and stung his eyes. The entire hall had seemed ablaze; he'd felt as if he stood inside a gigantic hearth as the smoke spiraled up the staircase into every lofty chamber.

He had been on the stairs, fighting like a madman to

keep anyone from gaining access to the rooms above. With him were Peter and Raven, all of them swinging their swords blindly as the swirling gray smoke diminished their vision. He had just defeated his latest opponent with a lethal sword thrust and stood propped against the wall gasping for breath when Sir Christian, captain of the guards, made his way up to him.

In his childhood room again, Lucien mouthed the captain's words, for he heard them clearly in his mind: "Lord Gundulf's dead, lads. Your father's dead, taken an arrow in the chest. 'Tis lost, it is. Eynsham is lost!"

For a slim moment Lucien had been confused. *He* was the lord, then, Eynsham's lord. Yet Sir Christian was declaring it lost. There was no time to think, to sort matters out. The captain rushed on, advising him and his brothers that Eynsham's knights were falling, either to the sword or in surrender. Soon enough Osric would declare the keep his own and demand fealty from one and all. Their only chance, Christian told them, was to flee the keep immediately. The smoke inside and the chaos in the yard would provide cover until they were beyond the walls.

They hesitated, the three of them. But all were young, barely old enough to be called men. When Christian, a man who had befriended them as children, who had pledged to give his life's blood for Eynsham, waved his sword above his head and shouted, "Go to it, lads!" instinctively they obeyed him and ran.

All the brothers recognized their defeat, but only Lucien knew the tearing sting of it. Neither he nor Peter and Raven felt anything like affection toward their sire; his death pricked them not. And all three had spent more years away from Eynsham, fostering with Becknock, than they had living in their sire's stronghold. But only Lucien felt the impact of becoming the lord of the keep and losing it, all within the space of a heartbeat.

Still, he went with Raven and Peter, all three groping their way through the hall and on outside, where they took the first mounts they came upon and escaped with nothing save the saddles beneath them.

"Jesu!" Lucien growled now, sitting up and glaring at the wall before him. "I was not a young pup who fled you in terror," he told Osric, though the old lord was only in the chamber because his image burned in Lucien's mind. "I escaped so that I might return and fight another day. That day is coming," he warned the man who appeared clearer to him than the nicked and faded furnishings that filled the small room. "And I am already here."

In a chamber above the one Lucien occupied, Charlotte soaked away the grime collected on her recent journey. Adrienne, who had already used the leaky wooden tub, knelt behind it, washing her sister's long, dark hair in a separate bucket.

"Addy," Charlotte said softly, the back of her neck resting on the rim of the tub. "Forgive me."

"Forgive you? Whatever for?"

"For . . . failing you."

"You've never failed me." Briskly, Adrienne soaped Charlotte's heavy mane of hair.

"But I did! When . . . when those men attacked us, I was frightened senseless. I knew one or both would force themselves on us. I knew that we would die if we did not try to defend ourselves. Yet I did nothing, I made not the slightest attempt to try and save us."

"Lottie." Adrienne rinsed the lather from her sister's tresses. "Do not speak of this now. 'Tis best we forget."

"Addy, I must!" Charlotte sat forward, her wet hair clinging to her naked back. "When the outlaw who held me raised my skirts . . . Oh, Adrienne, after that everything seemed to go black! I was powerless to move, powerless even to think!"

"I understand." Gently, she reached out to touch her shoulder.

"You don't!" Wrenching away, Charlotte turned to face Adrienne with wide, woeful eyes. "You cannot! 'Twas as if . . . as if I were already dead. I wished I *were* dead!" She paused, inhaling a ragged breath. "Then he shoved me aside, and—and—"

Tears that had been pooling in her eyes began to spill down her cheeks. Her voice sounded raw and hoarse as she admitted, "I heard all you said, Adrienne. I knew you intended to sacrifice yourself for my sake. As well I realized that neither of our attackers paid me any heed. I—I should have grabbed something—a rock, a fallen tree limb, anything—and clubbed one of the men senseless. But . . ." She shook her head slowly, as though in disbelief. "But I couldn't. I could do nothing at all."

"Charlotte, don't." Scrambling to her, Adrienne embraced Charlotte, oblivious to how her sister's wet body dampened her own, dry bed robe. "I do understand, truly. And it matters not. We both survived unscathed."

"It does matter! When you needed my help, I did nothing to aid you. I shall never forget it, Addy. And I vow I shall make it up to you someday, somehow, in some way."

"Lottie." Adrienne's voice was firm as she leaned away from the tub, her hands braced on Charlotte's naked shoulders. "You must listen to me and believe what I say. There was naught either of us might have done to overpower those villains. Were it not for Lucien's timely rescue, we'd neither of us be here now. Not at Eynsham. Not alive."

"Lucien." Charlotte repeated his name thoughtfully as she stepped out of the tub and snatched up a drying cloth. "I still find it awesome to know that he is a knight in King Henry's service. Was it a great surprise to you also?"

"Yes." Adrienne sat on the edge of the bed the girls shared. "But not as much of a surprise as his, when he learned I am no peasant either, but a lady born and bred."

"Oh?" Charlotte shrugged on her robe and sat beside Adrienne as she began to towel dry her hair. "He wasn't pleased?"

"Ha!" Adrienne snorted and shook her head. "It would seem courting a lady is not in his plans. That would interfere with his personal quest, which is to retrieve some article stolen from him long ago. Nay, the honorable Sir Lucien is inclined only to woo and to bed common wenches, whom he can easily forget when he rides away."

"Adrienne! Sweet Mother Mary, did you . . . ?"

"Nay." She turned to face Charlotte more squarely and took both her hands in her own. "I did nothing I regret. Yet I was taken with him," she admitted. A very small admission, she knew, considering the whole of the secret that now dwelled within her breast. "It pricked my pride, 'tis all, that he only showed some interest in me when he thought I was no more than a villein's daughter."

"Addy, he *is* interested in you. Else why is he here? And why did he help us—you—concoct that story for Grandfather? He did it because he cares for you and is trying to protect you."

"Hmph. It is not as if Grandfather would have beaten us, even if he'd found out the truth."

"Sir Lucien doesn't know that. And I think," Charlotte hurried on, looking thoughtfully at Adrienne, "that he accepted our guardian's invitation in order to spend some time with you. Mayhap he is even considering asking for your hand."

"Why should I want him to ask for my hand?" Adrienne demanded, leaping to her feet and striding away. "I have no interest in him or any man."

"No? Well, I think you should. Better to choose your

own husband for love than to have one forced on you for other reasons."

"Who is forcing . . . ?" Adrienne frowned as she faced her sister again. "Oh, Grandfather. Well, he has yet to follow through on his promise to secure us husbands. There's time yet."

"Oh?" Charlotte ran her fingernails through her damp, dark locks. "I would wager there's not so much time as you believe. Why do you think Lord Wilfred is here at Eynsham?"

A knot tightened in the pit of Adrienne's stomach as she recalled the man. "He did mention Grandfather's intention to see us wed soon, didn't he?" she remembered aloud as she sat down again. "I didn't like him. Did you?"

Charlotte hesitated a moment, and she chose her words carefully when she replied, "I did not dislike him. But as I've always been hopeful of joining a convent, I've not much formed an opinion of men, the sort I like and the sort I don't. I will give it some time before I judge Wilfred."

"I need no more time. I dislike him. I dislike all men!" Adrienne waved her arms dramatically.

Charlotte smiled a little smile and shook her head. "Nay, that's not true."

"It is."

"It is not. You loved our father, George of Brent, and Edward our stepfather. Certainly you care for Grandfather Osric."

"That is not the sort of "like" and "dislike" we are speaking of, Lottie."

She shrugged. "Some men are our fathers or brothers, our uncles or sons, but most become husbands to other women. I doubt one is very much different from another."

"Well, they ought to be. A husband should be a special sort, someone kind and caring, whom you'd be glad to have as the father of your children."

"You don't think Sir Lucien is special?"

Adrienne felt a tug in the region of her heart, yet stubbornly she replied, "Perhaps to some other lady. Not to me."

Charlotte didn't argue, and no more was said on the subject. But her silence did not mean she believed a word her sister spoke.

In the great hall below, Osric sat with Wilfred, both of them ignoring the noise and the bustle of the servants setting up trestle tables for the evening's meal. "Well, what do you think?" Osric asked his friend.

"Of Eynsham? 'Tis improved, I admit, since I saw it first that day we attacked Gundulf and took it from his family. The village has grown, and you've fortified the bailey walls with both bricks and mortar. You have more guards than even a king requires."

"Do not make light of my precautions," Osric warned, sipping from his mug of ale before wiping his lips on the back of his hand. "Gundulf left behind three sons. Anyone could recruit an army to attack me."

"I told you I heard his twin sons each have fees near Fortengall. Their mother, Gundulf's widow, wed the earl of Fortengall, did she not? In any event, neither would bother with this estate when each has his own demesne with a new-built keep." Wilfred set his own mug, empty, on the dais table.

"But the twins were not the eldest living. Neither you nor I has had word on the surviving firstborn's whereabouts."

"True." Wilfred nodded. "But if he has no land near his brothers', surely he is elsewhere in the kingdom, if indeed he still lives. And after all these years, he must have given up the idea of retaking Eynsham, if ever he had it."

"It took me more than a score of years before I came to take Eynsham."

"Also true. But the man's probably dead, slain in battle across the Channel somewhere, fighting another lord's war." Wilfred leaned his head against the high back of his carved chair. "What was he called?"

"I'm not certain. I think I heard Gundulf named his heir Lucien."

"Lucien?" Wilfred sat forward again. "Same as the knight who escorted your wards home?"

Osric frowned, his brows knitting together until they formed a single, fuzzy line above his eyes. "Aye," he confirmed, slowly nodding his head. "But there are as many Luciens in England as there are Georges and Johns. Besides, the young knight upstairs could not be he. To begin, if he were Gundulf's whelp, he'd not be bold enough to walk through my front portal. There's his looks, too. He has reddish hair and light eyes while my cousin was as dark as the devil, his hair and eyes as black as pitch. Then there are my wards to consider. Neither Adrienne nor Charlotte is inclined to tell falsehoods. If they claim to have known this knight of Henry's since childhood, they certainly have.

"Ach!" With a quick shake of his head, Osric topped off his mug and downed a mighty gulp of brew. "I have always been vigilant. But I'll not go looking for assassins in the shadows."

"You mentioned your faith in the young women you elected to regard as your kin," Wilfred observed as he leaned forward now, his elbows on the table. "Yet they are not your blood, only your son Edward's stepdaughters."

"I made them my kin when I made them my heirs. They are fine girls, not only pleasing to the eye but with a purity of soul." Osric's eyes narrowed. "When earlier I asked for your thoughts, I referred to Charlotte and Adrienne. How do you find them, Wilfred?"

Tenting his fingers under his chin, he replied, "They are both, as you say, exceedingly comely. You have amazing good luck to find yourself with marriageable granddaughters when your only child died without issue."

"Not lucky," Osric countered. "I'd have been lucky had my son lived, or if he and his wife had had children of their own. But I'll not complain. It was good fortune that the girls found their way here after Edward and Anne died. Now, at least, I have a sound chance of having male descendants to whom Eynsham will pass when I die."

"Aye, and for me, heirs to Houghton, since I—like you—have lost both my spouse and my offspring to pestilence. I need to beget new heirs to Houghton."

"And to Eynsham?"

"To Eynsham also." Wilfred chuckled, a gleam in his eye. " 'Tis not a sorry situation for a man to be in when he is responsible for siring enough children to inherit more than one estate. His work is his pleasure." He eyed Osric speculatively. "But you, my old friend? I must wonder why you don't wed again and try for more sons of your own."

"Never." The old lord shook his head and frowned. "Millicent died so many years ago, I've been alone too long. Now I am aged and too set in my ways to take a young bride. But you," he said, pointing at Wilfred, "you are a score of years younger than I and still have what it takes to make a wench mewl when you plow her. So, which of my granddaughters do you wish to wed?"

Wilfred smiled at nothing, though seeing him, one could

imagine that he was famished and that a succulent roasted swan had been set out on the table before him.

"I have only just met them, and briefly. It is too soon for me to make a decision. I must get to know each ... more intimately."

Chapter 10

Lucien entered the great hall unobserved. Osric and his friend already sat at the high table, their heads close together as they engaged in earnest conversation; servants scurried about, laying tables for the lord and his men. But neither Adrienne nor Charlotte was yet in attendance.

Pausing at the foot of the stairs, Lucien took in the room. He had sensed it before, but now he knew for certain. It had changed. Though the main chamber remained cramped and crowded as it had always been, Osric's hand on it was visible, Gundulf's all but erased.

Which, Lucien admitted to himself with great reluctance, was no bad thing. Gundulf had cared not at all for the state of his abode. He had entertained only other hard, cruel men like himself, men who would as soon stab you as argue with you, men who would drink 'til they puked on another's feet instead of their own, men who took their ease with unwilling wenches more often than with those few who were willing.

Lucien recalled that his mother had tried to make the keep a home for herself and her children, but with slim success. His father always returned from his travels to ridicule the efforts she made during his absence. He would casually toss food scraps onto the fresh rushes, or allow the hounds free rein to defecate where servants made their beds on the floor at night. Worse, the former lord of Eynsham would put a boot to Lucinda's backside when she bent over. Kicking her hard, Gundulf would send her sprawling. Or he would backhand her, cursing her in front of the strangers who'd returned to Eynsham with him, humiliating her and embarrassing his sons. Lucien had seen it all when he was a young boy, but he had not forgotten.

He *had* forgotten how dusty the stuffed stag heads had been, how faded and mildewed the wall hangings used to be, and how soot-blackened the stones behind the torches. But as he stood in the shadows noting the glistening fur on the trophies, the brilliant hues of the tapestries, and the scrubbed wall stones, it came back to him, how it once had been.

Lucien's eyes slid to his smiling foe, who remained as unaware of him as he was of the disaster looming. Lucien could not yet compliment Osric on the improvements he had made to Eynsham. But directly before he slew him, Lucien decided, he would thank the usurper for his efforts.

Adrienne spied Lucien standing at the foot of the stairs when she and Charlotte made their way down to the great hall. Lost in his thoughts, unaware of her presence, he appeared to her as she had never before seen him. Neither suave and seductive nor fearsome and strong, Lucien seemed very alone and a little sad.

Her first instinct was to go to him, to slip her hand into

his. But her second thought was not instinct at all, and it restrained her from making any impulsive moves. He regretted being her first lover, and his regret still stung her like a raw, wet wound. It did not matter much that he had abetted her in the making of the tale she'd told her guardian. It was not salve enough to heal her or to make her forgive him.

Adrienne stopped abruptly on one of the lower stone steps. Charlotte, following close behind, bumped into her. At the sound she made, Lucien turned and looked up at them.

For a moment, his and Adrienne's eyes locked. Then he stepped nearer, reached out, and offered her his hand.

"Welcome!"

Adrienne blinked, startled out of her reverie at the sound of Osric's booming voice. The three of them were approaching the dais, and though Charlotte's fingers rested lightly on Lucien's other elbow, Adrienne felt as though she'd been caught clinging to her lover. She pulled her own hand free from the crook of his arm and stepped onto the platform, taking her usual seat. Lucien took the one on her left, Charlotte the one on her right.

"Just in time," Osric continued. "Food's being served this very moment."

Servants indeed toted in victuals from the kitchen, platters and trays heaped high, bowls and tureens filled to their brims. All were set on the table until the boards fairly creaked under the weight. But though the men filled their bread trenchers and dove into their food with hearty appetites, Adrienne discovered she had no appetite at all. By comparison, Charlotte, who ate like a bird, put her to shame.

"Tell us of Carrington Fair," Osric ordered, startling

Adrienne once again. The old lord frowned at her as he hacked a sizable portion of meat from the bone of a leg of lamb. "Something weighty on your mind, Adrienne?"

"What? No, of course not," she lied. "What is it you'd like to know about the fair?"

"What you did and what you saw, of course." He peppered an egg before stuffing it, whole, into his mouth.

"Well." She glanced quickly at her sister and at Lucien, hesitating only a few moments more as she gulped a long draught of wine. "Have you ever been to Carrington Fair, Grandfather?"

"Nay, I have not."

"Oh!" Relieved to hear it, her forced smile suddenly became genuine. "It is a grand fair. I think Lottie and . . . Sir Lucien . . . would agree. Though, of course, Lottie and I have not been to so many that we've much to compare it with. But there were jugglers, acrobats, and minstrels."

"And a mystery play," Charlotte added helpfully.

"Oh, aye, a mystery play. There was also a . . . a—"

"—A fine horse auction."

Adrienne exhaled a sigh of relief at Lucien's unbidden remark. She glanced at him furtively before looking back at her grandfather. "That's true," she agreed, "though Lottie and I had no real interest in it. Oh! I bought the prettiest chaplet, Grandfather. 'Tis made of fresh flowers and embroidered ribands . . ."

Now that she had begun, Adrienne found it impossible to stop or even slow down. Her words tumbled out in a rush as she described the fair, which, in truth, had been Fortengall Fair, not the nearer one in Carrington. But she was not a stupid girl, and she realized that one must be very much like another, so she embellished her recounting with elaborate detail. It seemed to please her guardian.

"Did you compete in any tourneys, Sir Lucien?" Wilfred

asked when Adrienne paused to draw a deep breath and sip some refreshment.

"Nay, I did not. 'Twas a bit of leisure for me, my time at the fair. To have jousted would have seemed too much like work."

"How long have you served King Henry?"

Lucien shrugged. "Since shortly after I was knighted. He had a need for a complement of permanent guards, so I offered my sword arm and he accepted."

Adrienne, no longer the focus of everyone else's attention, allowed herself to gaze at Lucien's profile. Despite the fact that she knew she shouldn't care, she remained curious about him. Now she felt hopeful that he might possibly divulge some details, perhaps even speak of his quest.

"I have seen Henry's castle at Vouvant," Wilfred announced, enabling all at the table to see the whitefish swimming between his molars.

"King Henry has no castle at Vouvant," Lucien corrected him as he sat back nonchalantly in his chair. "Nay, the nearest our sovereign calls home is at Niort."

"Oh, yes. I stand corrected," Wilfred admitted, wiping his lips on his sleeve.

"How long has it been since you left his court?"

Osric asked the question, and Adrienne's eyes leapt to the old man's face. She peered at him curiously, sensing a sudden change in the tone of conversation.

"Some weeks now," Lucien replied.

"Have you any news?"

"Grandfather," Adrienne interrupted. "It would likely be improper for Sir Lucien to tell tales of the royal court."

"Nonsense. Everyone spreads gossip about the king and queen and their retinue. Isn't that so?" His eyes slid from his ward to his guest.

"I believe it is."

"What's the news, then?"

Lucien sat forward in his chair, propping his elbows on the table and resting his chin on his folded hands. "King Henry has just made Thomas of Becket the Archbishop of Canterbury."

"What!"

"Shrewd," Wilfred commented, arching his brows as he nodded his head in approval.

"The Church hierarchy must be mutinous. Becket's not even a priest!" Osric snorted.

"He is now. Becket was ordained the day before Henry named him Archbishop."

"Shrewd," Wilfred said again. "Now Henry has a man in his pouch who heads both the secular and divine posts. How clever of him to arrange it."

"King Henry is very clever. Perhaps too clever, for this time he may have outwitted himself."

"How so?"

Lucien sighed and dropped his hands into his lap. "Upon becoming archbishop, Becket resigned all his secular posts. He seems not to be of a mind with our sovereign, and he follows his own mind."

"God's bones!" Osric exclaimed. "Becket will find his head separated from his body for this."

"Nay." Lucien shook his head. "Henry is not that sort. A good man he is, and fair."

"Has it something to do with Becket that you're on Saxon soil instead of across the Channel with the king?"

"Grandfather!" Adrienne interrupted again. "Lucien may find all these questions impertinent!"

Though she'd spoken up for his benefit, Lucien ignored her. Retrieving a parchment from the leather pouch on his belt, he unrolled the narrow scroll as he told Osric and Wilfred, "I fear I cannot divulge the purpose of my being here. But 'tis of the utmost importance, I assure you."

Everyone seated caught a glimpse of the Plantagenet seal at the bottom of the document, but Adrienne noticed as well the slight smile quirking a corner of Lucien's mouth. The rest seemed satisfied that he was, indeed, on some business involving King Henry and the new archbishop, but Adrienne wondered if there wasn't something more, something else.

That topic quickly came to a close, but others rose up in its place. The men discussed hunting, horses, and hawks; Adrienne and Charlotte listened until they grew bored, and then they stopped listening.

"Which of you ladies would like to escort me to Evandale on the morn?" Wilfred asked abruptly, catching both sisters unaware. Their heads popped up, and they stared at him as though they were watching some sea serpent push its head above the crested waves.

"I returned with your—your grandsire to Eynsham to see what he'd done with the fee since it came into his hands. But with you two gone missing, I've been delayed on that score. I should like to see the village. Which of you would like to show it to me?"

"Lady Adrienne has already pledged to take me about," Lucien announced.

Startled, she blinked at him.

"I'd like . . . very much . . . to show you Evandale," Charlotte said softly.

Adrienne's head snapped to the other side, her expression one of total disbelief. "Mayhap we could all go," she volunteered.

"Nay, Addy. I should like very much to . . . have the pleasure of . . . showing Lord Wilfred anything he would like to see here at Eynsham or in Evandale. You—you accompany Sir Lucien."

"Good. It's all settled then," Osric declared, smiling broadly.

"Aye." Charlotte pushed back her chair. "But if you will all excuse me, I confess to being very tired. The last days have been . . . exhausting."

As she rose, Adrienne stood also. "I, too," she admitted. "I fear I must seek my bed."

Wilfred smiled at the girls, his smile bordering on a leer. "Would you like me to escort you both to your bed . . . chamber?"

"I'll escort them." Lucien leapt to his feet. "I'm short on sleep myself, and my room is near theirs, so you needn't disturb yourself, Lord Wilfred. Goodnight."

In silence, the three left the hall, and in silence they climbed the circular stairs. On the landing beyond the sisters' bedchamber, they all halted. Charlotte pushed open the door but turned to look up at Lucien.

"My lord," Charlotte whispered softly, "I fear I've been remiss in offering you my thanks. Most of all for rescuing us on the road 'twixt Fortengall and Eynsham, but also for helping us—well, Adrienne, actually—to spin the tale that spared us from having to tell our grandfather the truth of our folly."

"It was my pleasure. Although . . ." He frowned thoughtfully at the brown-eyed beauty who seemed as reserved and pious as the Holy Mother must have been.

"Yes?"

"Unlike your sister, I'd not have thought you would choose a lie over the truth, no matter what the circumstances."

"Oh—you!" Adrienne gasped, insulted. But Lucien ignored her, keeping his attention entirely devoted to Charlotte.

She also sputtered, momentarily at a loss for words. Blushing in the same fashion Adrienne frequently did, Charlotte finally managed to choke out, "Sir! Of course I believe speaking falsehoods is terribly wrong and most always sinful. But—'' She glanced at her sister before looking back at Lucien. "Sometimes there are exceptions. To spare another's feelings, perhaps, or—"

"To avoid the brutal wrath of one who might harm you?" he suggested.

This time Charlotte's mouth merely opened and closed. Though she blinked at him with wide eyes, she said nothing at all.

Lucien discovered Adrienne had no such problem.

"How dare you speak to Lottie that way," she hissed at him. "Implying our grandfather is some mean ogre we should fear! Who are you to make such judgments? You may be a knight in royal service, but you are not the king!"

"Addy, please." Charlotte wrung her hands. "Keep your voice down. Someone might overhear."

It dismayed Lucien to see how distraught she'd become. "I apologize," he said quickly, taking one of Charlotte's hands and brushing her knuckles with a chaste kiss. "I'd no business saying what I did. I'm pleased to have been of assistance to you in whatever manner I could."

She smiled a tight little smile and gave him a curt little nod before backing over the threshold into her room. "I'm going to bed now. Rest well, Sir Lucien."

"I'm coming, too." Adrienne graced Lucien with a withering glare and attempted to follow her sister.

But Lucien grabbed her elbow and held her back. "I think not," he announced. "I should like to speak with you further."

"I believe we've said all we could ever have to say to each other."

"Oh? I thought we should plan our next story in advance this time, so we need not invent it on the spot. Too risky, that."

Adrienne's eyes sparkled like hoarfrost. Her beauty came as much from within as without, and it glowed with her passions, be they lust or fury. Lucien found it impossible not to be entertained as he watched her conflicts play out across her face.

"If we must discuss our stories, then Lottie should be included." Adrienne wrenched her elbow free.

"Nay, you don't need me," Charlotte insisted as she took another step into the bedchamber. "Addy, you can tell me whatever you've agreed upon."

"There's nothing to agree upon!" She swung back toward Lucien. "The business of our sneaking off to the fair is done. Grandfather accepts what we have told him. There'll be no more mention of it."

"I prefer to take no more chances. Goodnight, Lady Charlotte." He nodded to her as she slowly closed the door, leaving her sister on the landing. Then he grabbed Adrienne's elbow again, and he propelled her up the stairs before him, all the way to the top room in the keep, the solar.

Inside the large, windowed chamber, Lucien snatched a candle and returned to the staircase where he lit its wick from a torch's flame. Stubbornly, Adrienne remained outside the door, though he noticed she did not use her freedom to retreat down the stairs. When he had lighted several candles in the solar from his one burning flame, he reached through the doorway, took her hand, yanked her forcibly inside the room, and closed the door behind them.

"Why are you so angry?" he asked, giving her his back as he strolled to the high, wide window and sat on the cushioned seat just below it.

Adrienne set her chin and clutched her arms, which she folded across her bosom. "Because," she replied as Lucien crossed his legs casually and graced her with a level gaze, "you insulted my sister. How dare you suggest she's a liar? Lottie's the most honest, honorable, pious, obedient woman I've ever known! She was even schooled for some years in a convent."

Lucien smiled at Adrienne. "Were you? Convent-schooled, I mean."

"Why?"

"My guess is you weren't."

"You!" Her arms flew out, hands clenched, as she strode toward him. Yet she stopped in the middle of the room, as though reluctant to get too near him.

"I wasn't insulting you." Lucien came to his feet but did not approach Adrienne. " 'Tis only I've observed you are very headstrong and willful, and not inclined to take orders from anyone. Unlike Charlotte, I doubt you could have endured living with a convent of nuns."

"Well, I didn't. I didn't even like it much when I visited Lottie there."

Adrienne's chin had dropped a little. Now it came up again, and she took another step toward Lucien. "Why would you suggest such vile things about our grandfather? That he is brutal and wrathful, I believe you said. He invited you to stay here, Lucien. He offered you his hospitality!"

"And he took you two in when your parents died, but I surmised you feared that he would find out about your excursion to Fortengall. Why, Addy?" Lucien asked softly as he strolled slowly toward her. "Why, if you did not fear his heavy hand?"

He stood near enough now that he could see her face soften from its hard lines of anger into gentle planes and curves.

"Do you think Osric beats us? Or that he forces us into drudgery?" She shook her head. "Lucien, he does not. He's been naught but good to us since our parents died of the pox in the high heat of last summer."

"Then why did you leave without telling him? Why were you so glad not to have to confess where you'd gone?"

"Because what we did was wrong, and it nearly cost us our lives, as you well know. We'd no wish for him to know we repaid his many kindnesses with such foolery. At least, I did not," Adrienne elaborated, "for it was all my doing. And Lottie would have been forced to share the blame."

For a moment, the two were silent, Lucien feeling himself falling into the depths of Adrienne's bright blue eyes while she steeled herself to keep from being swamped by Lucien's green-eyed gaze. When he reached out and cupped her cheek in his hand, he felt her jaw clench and saw her shoulders stiffen.

"Why are you here?"

"What?" He dropped his hand to his side.

"Why are you here? Escorting us home to Eynsham surely delayed you, if it didn't take you out of your way. You do appear to be on some sort of mission, either for your king or yourself. Why, then, do you tarry at this humble keep?"

"I—" Lucien's black brows knit together above his nose as he frowned in consternation.

"Has it to do with your personal quest?"

"What!" It was his turn, now, to stiffen his shoulders.

"Is it a woman you're after?" Adrienne pressed. "Does she reside near here, perhaps at Cox or Widdenham? Is she some other man's wife?"

"Christ, no!"

"Then what possible reason could you have for remaining here when you had no intention of coming here in the first place?"

"You!" The syllable on his lips sounded more a primitive growl than a recognizable word as he reached out again, this time with both hands and this time grabbing Adrienne's shoulders. As he drew her to him, he confessed, "I am here because of you!"

It was no lie. True, Adrienne had been like a charm,

the key to unlocking Eynsham's gate. But even more important, it was she, the damsel herself, whom Lucien found himself reluctant to leave. Now, he wanted her—every smooth, rounded curve, every moist, musky crevice. His cock hurt, straining in his braies to be freed and trapped elsewhere all over again.

He relaxed his fingers and moved his hands along her shoulders and neck until his thumbs rested against her rosy cheeks. When he had her face imprisoned, Lucien lowered his to hers and pressed a gentle, sensual, drawing kiss upon her lips.

He heard Adrienne whimper, a tiny sound deep in her throat. He felt her begin to lean into him, those two pert nubs crowning each of her breasts poking her bliaut and grazing his tunic tantalizingly.

But in the next instant she shook her head and pulled away. Though her lips were kiss-swollen and she licked them provocatively, Adrienne snapped, " 'Tis a lie, sir! You made it clear you've no interest in me, nor would you ever have, had you known I was a virginal lady, not an overripe peasant ready for swiving!"

"Lady or not, you were ready for swiving!"

Lucien grabbed Adrienne again. This time his kiss was as demanding as it was possessive. He could feel her teeth through her lips, yet he drew her closer, fists in her hair, and rubbed his swollen sex against her belly.

With dexterous fingers, he unlaced the sides of her bliaut and the back of her undertunic. As his lips traced a path from Adrienne's ear to her collar bone, he pulled the shoulders of her garments down one arm, exposing a full, pink-tipped breast. His head burrowed lower to suckle on that nut-hard nipple, and he dragged up the hem of her gown to run his fingers up her soft, sensitive inner thighs until they found what they truly sought.

She was wet, and her breath in his ear sounded labored.

But the moment his fingertips touched the folded petals between her legs, Adrienne cried out and lurched away. Scrambling to regain her balance by leaning against a sturdy table, she yanked up her fallen sleeve and covered her naked breast.

Lucien watched her reassemble herself as he tried to slow his own ragged breathing. He thought he might burst if he could not get himself inside her soon. He wanted her; nay, needed her. Jesu! he found himself thinking desperately, if only she would consent to be my mistress yet!

But Adrienne was speaking of marriage. The word flickered like a firefly, caught his attention and disappeared. Like a drunken fool attempting to regain his wits, Lucien blinked repeatedly, trying to focus on Adrienne and what she was saying.

"I am no peasant girl, no daughter of a serf tied to another's land. I am the daughter of a landed knight and his lady, granddaughter to the lord of this keep. And that lord wants me wed soon." She inhaled a deep breath as Lucien's eyes followed the rise and fall of her loosely covered breasts. "Well?"

"Well . . . what?"

"Damn you!" Adrienne shouted.

"No." He shook his head confusedly. "I did not hear all of what you said, Addy. What . . .?"

"Do you intend to ask for my hand?" she repeated, pushing herself away from the table and coming a step toward him.

If she had just plunged a small dagger into his chest, Lucien could not have been more surprised. But he sobered from his love-drunkenness quickly enough, his chest puffing up with a deeply inhaled breath even as his sex deflated.

"I cannot." His tone was firm. "If I could, I would, Addy. But it is impossible."

"It cannot be your service to the king that prevents you from marrying," she surmised. "Are you already wed?"

"Nay!"

"Is it your quest?"

"Aye. My quest." *And the fact that we are cousins sharing a common ancestor, Ranulf, grandfather to Gundulf and Osric. Short a generation on my side, the Church would surely rule us too close by blood to sanctify a formal union between us.*

"Where are you going?" he demanded.

Adrienne was tying her strings even as she strode toward the solar door.

"Away from you," she informed him without even turning to look at him over her shoulder. "I shall be some lord's bride soon enough, and I do not care to compromise myself further. Not with the likes of you," she added as she pulled open the door.

"You can't avoid me while I'm here. On the morrow you're to take me on a tour of the keep, the grounds."

She hesitated at the threshold, but still did not look back. When she left, though, she left in silence. By not saying nay, she had as good as agreed to uphold her promise.

Alone, Lucien scowled. He'd best learn all he need to on the morrow, he decided, so that he could be gone from Eynsham Keep quickly. It would be unfairly hard on Addy if he remained too long.

But it would be even worse for him.

Chapter 11

The ladies were in their room, Charlotte plaiting Adrienne's hair. "How did things go with you and Lucien last eve?"

"You were there, Lottie."

"I was not." She gave her sister's hair a tug. "Did you and Lucien go up to the solar? Did you concoct another story? I do so hate telling Grandfather tales."

"When we first returned home, we had no choice," Adrienne insisted. "And as you refused to join Lucien and me, I assumed you were not very interested in any new story we devised."

"I am! But I thought you'd share it with me now."

"There's truly naught to share. 'Tis as I said last eve: Grandfather has accepted what we've told him. There's no need to tell more lies."

"I fell asleep before you returned, so you must have

been gone awhile. What did you speak of then, if not another fabrication to tell Grandfather?"

"Marriage."

Charlotte tied off Adrienne's second braid and spun her around on her stool so that they faced each other. "Lucien asked you to marry him?"

"No. Lucien told me he could not."

"Oh." Charlotte's excitement melted away like glittering snow on a warm, spring day. But next she smiled a sunny smile. "It is on his mind, though. It must be, for him to have mentioned the matter. Perhaps he'll reverse his decision if his circumstances change."

With her foot, Adrienne pulled herself around on her stool, giving Charlotte her back again. She would not admit that she herself had broached the subject. If Charlotte knew everything she had done of late and that she'd nearly succumbed to Lucien's seducing ways again, her sister would be both shocked and ashamed. Adrienne could not have borne her sister's pity.

"I've told you before," Adrienne said, coming to her feet, "I've no interest in Lucien or any man. But you," she spun around on the balls of her feet, "you are interested in Lord Wilfred?"

Charlotte's delicate chin dropped to her breast. "I may be. I don't know him well enough yet."

Adrienne held her tongue, deciding it more prudent to refrain from reiterating her own dislike of Wilfred, a dislike her sister did not seem to share. Instead, pursing her lips thoughtfully, she appraised Charlotte's garb. "It appears he's already interested in you, Lottie. But it might help if you dressed more prettily. The bliaut you've donned is the color of pig shite."

"Adrienne! How can you speak so?"

Returning Charlotte's horrified gasp with a giggle, she declared, "Because it's true! By the heavenly saints, Lottie, where did you find such a hideous tunic? Did you borrow it from the butcher's wife?"

"Nay! I used to wear it at the monastery." Glancing down at her skirts she added, "It's serviceable still."

"Aye. As a scrub rag."

"But Lord Wilfred and I will be riding today. I don't wish to ruin any of my nicer gowns."

"If they get dirtied, we'll launder them. Wear something of a hue that flatters your hair and your complexion."

"If we stay fairly long in town, mayhap we won't ride too much," Charlotte suggested as she untied her bliaut laces.

"Most likely you won't. And this will do nicely," Adrienne announced, retrieving a bliaut and undertunic of two varying shades of rose from her sister's clothes chest. "The colors will put a bloom in your cheeks and sparkle in your eyes. You'll get your man by looking like a flower, not a mouse."

Charlotte was all but hidden as Adrienne spoke, caught up in the tunic she was tugging off. But when her head popped free, she looked peaked, not flushed.

Adrienne didn't notice as she handed her the fresh gowns. "I do hope you find yourself happily wed soon. To Wilfred, if he is your choice."

"Oh, Addy. 'Tis you I wish to see happy in marriage! You've always dreamed of it."

Her sister's weepy tone was impossible to overlook. Surprised by it, Adrienne caught Charlotte up in an impulsive hug. "Just because there's no man yet who's caught my eye does not mean one won't come along soon." Gently, she pushed Charlotte back. "But if you are intrigued with Wilfred of Houghton, let's make you ready to intrigue him.

"Oh, my," she sighed a minute later. "Lady Charlotte, you are indeed beautiful."

* * *

Lord Wilfred seconded Adrienne's opinion when the young women entered the great hall to join the men already seated, most of their morning's repast consumed. "You look beautiful this morn, both of you," Wilfred announced, though his eyes lingered on Charlotte before raking over Adrienne.

Charlotte muttered a thank-you and blushed, appearing uneasy. Adrienne ignored him and Lucien, too.

The young knight was not unaware of the lady's icy demeanor; she was like a cold wind gusting at him, pushing him back. And though he did not echo Wilfred's appraisal, he agreed with it. Adrienne more than her sister, he decided, looked exquisite this day in a turquoise bliaut trimmed with embroidered pink roses. Exactly like a strong wind, she fairly stole his breath away.

God's bloody wounds!

His more gentle musings scattered with that explosive exclamation, though he did not utter it aloud. Instead he speared a piece of pork with his knife as if the pig were still on the run. There had to be some way he could make Adrienne succumb to his charms again. If only once more. Just one more time of knowing her generous mouth, her thrusting breasts, and the feel of her warm, moist woman's flesh clutching him like a fitted glove . . .

"When will you four be setting out?" Osric asked, inadvertently stealing Lucien's attention from his own, private thoughts.

"Immediately." Wilfred smiled at Charlotte, who sat across from him.

"We, too," Lucien put in.

"I—" Adrienne gave him a loathful glance, as though he were a repugnant reptile. "I have some duties that require my attention. Perhaps later."

"Nonsense." Osric shook his balding head. "You've promised to show Sir Lucien about, and show him about you will. Whatever it is you must do, you can surely do later. One thing about work," he added confidentially, leaning across the table toward Lucien, "is that it never goes away no matter how long you delay it. Is that not so?"

The younger man nodded, chagrined that he had his enemy on his side.

Yet it seemed her grandsire's prodding worked to silence any objections Adrienne may have intended to voice. Though she refused to look directly at him again, Lucien saw her shrug resignedly.

"Should we be off?" Wilfred asked Charlotte.

The two rose from their chairs as Osric called out to one of his menservants. "Davey! See that Lord Wilfred's mount and a palfrey for Lady Charlotte are saddled immediately.

"And, Wilfred," he warned the man standing beside him, "see you do not consume too much of Evandale's brew mistress' ale this early in the day. 'Tis heady stuff, indeed."

"Your warning's well taken." With a wink that noticeably flustered Charlotte, Wilfred took that lady's hand and led her from the hall.

"Well, why are you dawdling?" Osric asked the two remaining. His tone was sharp; Lucien glanced at him expecting a scowl, but found, instead, a good-natured smile on the old lord's face. "The day's a-wasting and, I fear, I've responsibilities I can no longer ignore. I put them off overlong, involved as I was in searching for my granddaughters."

Though Osric teased her, Adrienne lowered her lashes guiltily. When he quit the room, however, her blue eyes snapped in Lucien's direction.

"I don't suppose," she said, "you could brave wandering about this keep and its bailey on your own?"

"I'd prefer a guide."

"I'd prefer you left Eynsham immediately."

Lucien turned in his chair and leaned back against the arm to better see her. She bristled like an angry hen, feathers mussed and flying. "Why would you want that?" he asked her.

"Because you should not be here. When first I met you, I did not intend to bring you home with me!"

"I'd wager that when first you met me, you did not intend to make love with me, either. But you did."

"Oooooh!" She stood so abruptly, she nearly pushed her chair off the dais. "And I thought you an honorable man. But then, I thought you a serf."

"I *am* honorable." Lucien leaped up and grabbed her arm, all in a lightning flash movement; his voice was a rough whisper that made Adrienne flinch. "But honorable men are sometimes forced to do dishonorable things."

For a moment, she felt startled and confused. Then her fury resurfaced, restrained only by her purposeful silence as Lucien led her not to the front portal, but into the kitchens and on through the postern door. Outside in the yard, Adrienne turned to him with a puzzled frown.

Before she even opened her mouth to speak, he realized what he had done.

"All keeps' sculleries have a door in near the same place," he explained quickly.

"I hardly think that's true."

"Well, 'twould seem to be true in this instance—at least as far as my own experience goes."

She squinted suspiciously but said no more. Stepping in front of him, she walked on as though intending to leave him behind. "What do you wish to see first?" she called back over her shoulder.

Had he said the armory, he would have spoken truly. But Lucien spied the mews and named it instead.

Without a backward glance at him, Adrienne headed to where the hawks were housed. Cutting a path through the bustling workers, she nodded, smiled, and greeted everyone she encountered along the way. Yet she did not deign to introduce Lucien.

He was glad. He needed no Eynsham laborers or servants to put his name and face together, only to realize he was the former lord's son.

In the mews, Lucien donned a leather glove and examined the jerfalcons, the merlins, and the goshawks. "Do you enjoy hawking, Lady Adrienne?"

"Nay." She folded her arms over her chest and gave her back to the birds as she watched the activity in the bailey. "Lottie and I grew up as farmer's daughters. 'Twas a large place, with servants and tenants to help us. But there was no time to be had for the leisurely sport of hawking."

He put the bird he'd been holding back on its perch. Removing the leather glove, Lucien walked around Adrienne and took her hands in his to examine them. "Ah, yes. Cracked, roughened, callused palms. No wonder you fooled me so well when I met you at Fortengall."

She pulled her soft hands away as though he'd scalded them. "You're making sport at my expense, but I am neither spoiled nor pampered. I know all a chatelaine must to run a household. As well, I could tell you when to plant and when to harvest." She paused, waiting for an apology that went unoffered. "Oh, you are cruel!"

"But when I love you, I love you well."

Adrienne's ivory skin turned a shade that matched the roses on her gown. Lucien's smile broadened as her color heightened. He was tempted to touch his lips to her cheeks to feel their sudden heat, but he restrained himself. Knowing his unwanted presence rattled her was nearly as good as having her succumb to his honeyed words and expert touch.

"Are you finished inspecting Eynsham's falcons?" she asked tartly. Not waiting for him to respond, she strode away from the birds' shelter, forcing Lucien to follow.

"That's the old chapel," she announced, stopping abruptly and pointing to the small, timbered structure. "No one uses it any longer, not since Grandfather had the new church built in Evandale."

"When did he do that?"

"Build the church?" She frowned. "I've no idea. Lottie and I have lived at Eynsham less than a twelve-month. Father Lawrence was already presiding over the church in the village when we arrived."

Adrienne resumed her walking. She no longer looked at the closed chapel, but then, neither did Lucien. The breeze had kicked up, and it made the very wide cuffs on her bliaut flutter like wings. It also pressed the fabric at her back against her bottom and thighs. Lucien admired the curve of her derriere and the line of her shapely legs. Impulsively, he took another step that brought him immediately beside her; he reached out with one hand, intending an intimate yet discreet caress. It was on his mind to lure Adrienne back into the keep and up to some secluded chamber, when she spoke.

"My sister and I have oft wondered when anyone had the time to build a new church, what with all the time spent on the walls."

"What?" Lucien's hand dropped to his side.

"Look!" Her own arms wide, Adrienne gestured to the walls enclosing the keep and its outbuildings. "Look how high they are. Grandfather is always ordering another row of stones to be cemented to the last. I'm surprised no one is working on it now. Mayhap," she added, "he's realized that another foot to those walls and even the solar window would be darkened by their shadow."

His plans for seduction again subsided, along with his sex, which had enjoyed a sudden spurt of growth. Lucien looked up at the crenelated parapets. On the ledge that ran along the inside of the bailey walls, three-fourths of a man's height from the top, dozens of bowmen paced and lounged as they surveyed the countryside beyond.

"Too many, don't you think?" Adrienne asked softly, as though she were privy to Lucien's unspoken thoughts. Before he might argue or agree, she continued, "Grandfather has such a large force protecting his keep, he had to build a barracks to house them. I've thought, after glimpsing the castle at Fortengall, he must have more men to protect Eynsham than the earl does his formidable stronghold."

"Who is it he fears?"

"Grandfather? Fear?" She scowled at Lucien as if he were a dolt. "Why, nothing and no one. The Lord of Eynsham is as strong and secure as his keep."

"Is he?" Lucien stepped in front of her and looked down into Adrienne's eyes. "Then tell me, my lady. Why the high walls and heavy guard?"

"Because he wants to be prepared," she explained, a hint of exasperation in her tone. " 'Tis weak and thoughtless land-lords who lose their estates to roving barons, or so my guardian's said to me. He loves Eynsham. He has no intention of losing it to anyone."

"Osric loves Eynsham?" Lucien scoffed, feeling the heat of his blood coursing through his veins. He himself loved Eynsham. The old impostor lord could know naught of such love—love of land and place, family and history. "I doubt he loves this small and unimportant demesne. Even the village is poor and unyielding. Besides, he has not ruled here long, has he? I heard it came to him as spoils from battle.''

"You misheard, sir! Eynsham was bequeathed to Lord Osric. It should have come to him while he was still in his youth. But some wicked cousin—Gundulf, I believe he was called—took possession before he could return to claim it.''

Lucien tensed at hearing his sire's name on Adrienne's lips. "Gundulf," he repeated.

"Aye. He was a brute who neglected his people and let both the town of Evandale and Eynsham Keep fall to ruin. But finally he died, and Grandfather at last acquired—''

"Acquired?''

"Acquired!'' she spat emphatically. "Gundulf died, and after a lapse of a score and five years, my guardian finally got what was due him. And he does love Eynsham, as though it were a woman he'd once loved and then lost and finally found again. 'Tis why he holds it so secure. If his efforts seem excessive, so be it. He does what he must, as do you.''

She reached up to fling a braid that had fallen across her breast back over her shoulder. Inadvertently, the end whipped Lucien's face, causing him to blink. Blinking seemed to clear his vision, and he saw Adrienne more clearly. She still cared for him! The smug satisfaction that knowledge gave him tempered his irritation at hearing Osric's distorted version of the truth.

"Addy," he said, grazing her jaw with his knuckles, "I would like things to be as they were between us. I never meant to upset you.''

"Nay?'' She slapped his hand away. "Then why are you still here? Why did you not decline my guardian's invitation? Why did you even bother escorting us home after you discovered I was not some randy peasant wench intent on bedding her first man?''

There were people everywhere, scurrying about, chattering. But to Lucien they seemed nothing but a blur of drab colors and a distant din. He and Adrienne might as well have been on some distant mountaintop. If they had been, he would have pulled her to him and smothered these familiar questions with kisses. But they were not, so he did what he could, given their circumstances. Moving toward her, he hooked one finger into the cord tied around Adrienne's waist. Instinctively, she leaned back to maintain her balance, which only brought her hips and belly closer to him.

"If I released you now, you'd fall," he whispered. "Best you hold on to me."

"I've no wish to hold on to you." Her eyes flashed. "I only wish that you'd leave!"

"You don't mean that. We've desired each other from the moment we first met. After all that's gone between us, you can only want me more, as I want you."

"Lucien."

Adrienne righted herself a little; her bosom brushed his chest. That touch ignited a spark that instantly resurrected his manhood.

"Please," she begged softly, wetting her parted lips in a way that made Lucien want to crush them beneath his own. "It is all changed now. We're no longer strangers, nor are we alone upon the road. This is my home. These are my people. My guardian—"

"Why do you call Osric your guardian?" Lucien interrupted, concerned that if he did not focus on something other than Adrienne's lush body and the sunlight sparkling upon her hair, he would embarrass himself like some randy squire. "True, he may be such in fact. But he is your grandsire first, isn't he?"

"Nay!" Her sooty lashes fluttered as she used her fingers to uncurl his from the cord at her waist. "Osric is not my true kin. He was father to Edward, my mother's second husband. My own father was George of Brent. Lottie and I had not even met Osric 'til after our parents—our mother and Edward—succumbed to the pox. But he took us in," she added, putting a little space between herself and Lucien. "And he made us his heirs, Eynsham our dower, so that the first son born to either me or Lottie will one day rule here."

"Sir Lucien!"

Silently he thanked whomever called his name, for the interruption spared him from looking as surprised as he felt. Turning toward the voice, both he and Adrienne saw the knight, Hubert, approaching.

"I understand you are touring the grounds this morn. I came to offer myself as your guide, if you are interested in seeing the armory, the barracks, and our routine of battle exercises on the training field." Hubert allowed his gaze to drift to Adrienne. "I realize, of course, I would be indifferent company compared to our lovely Lady Adrienne."

She smiled back at Hubert before looking again at Lucien—Lucien, who raised no objections to the knight's offer. Keeping her eyes locked on his, she said to Hubert, "I am certain our guest is most interested in viewing those knightly accommodations. As I am not, I gladly give him into your capable hands."

With a scowl that scorched Lucien before it cooled into a curt nod which dismissed Hubert, Adrienne turned on her heel. She then flounced off in the direction of the keep's rear door.

Lucien fell into step beside Hubert, who had already begun to enthusiastically describe the weaponry and skills it seemed only Eynsham's guard possessed. But he was not yet listening. Better than a peek into his enemy's stores, he had found the key to his victory: Addy, Lady Adrienne of Eynsham.

"Impressive, is it not?" Hubert asked, interrupting Lucien's contemplation. They had just reached the barracks.

"Aye," he agreed distractedly as he followed the Eynsham knight inside. Squinting to improve his vision in the sudden gloom, he did not see all that he might have. He did not see the man lounging in a corner, the man whose eyes were keenly focused on Eynsham's unexpected visitor.

Chapter 12

Adrienne had no real chores to do, not since she'd come to Eynsham. Osric unwittingly kept the two sisters idle by treating them as though they were guests. Thus, they occupied themselves with what amused them. Charlotte was inclined toward sewing when she wasn't at Evandale's church assisting Father Lawrence or studying the scriptures under his tutelage. Whenever a mare foaled, however, Adrienne would surely be found in the stables helping the men and the mare with the birth. She also kept a garden in which she grew vegetables and herbs; sometimes she helped Eynsham's cook, Hilda, concoct new recipes.

She had no real reason, then, to return to the keep after leaving Lucien. So though Adrienne did go to her bedchamber, almost immediately she whirled about and fled outdoors again, pausing only long enough to change her clothes. Within minutes she was at her garden near the rear of the bailey. She found it sadly in need of tending, her absence having left it vulnerable to sprawling weeds and nibbling rabbits. Glad for something to occupy her hands and her mind, Adrienne toted water from the well and eagerly fell to her knees to scrabble in the dirt.

Yet the hoped-for peace of mind and pleasant exhaustion that tending her plants usually brought her did not come. Adrienne's dark, churning emotions seemed to frighten them away, leaving her with only aching muscles and chipped nails to show for her toil.

"I hate him," she muttered as she yanked weeds from the stony soil. "He thought me little better than a slut; he used me for his pleasure and was done with me. Why does he remain here? Why doesn't he leave?"

She paused long enough to wipe a dark smudge across her brow with the back of one hand. "Holy Mother Mary! That Lottie would think I'd be pleased to take that arrogant, self-centered knight to husband! Ha! He can have his quest and his whores. I hope he grows old without having got back whatever they took from him, and that some dirty slattern gives him something that makes his peg rot off!"

The weeding and watering did not help at all; the muttered rantings only a little. Hours later, the garden neat and tended, Adrienne sweaty and begrimed, she returned to the keep in no better mood than she'd left it.

Encountering his ward in the great hall, Osric frowned disapprovingly when he saw her. "Adrienne! How come you to be so bedraggled? I thought you were accompanying your friend about the demesne, not making mud porridge with the servants' children."

Scowling petulantly, she planted her hands on her hips. "I was not making mud porridge, Grandfather. I was working in my garden."

Osric raised a questioning eyebrow.

"Sir Lucien seemed more inclined to have Sir Hubert

show him about," Adrienne explained. "They were talking military strategies and on their way to the guards' barracks when I left them."

For a long, thoughtful moment, the old lord considered the girl he deemed his granddaughter. Then he motioned for her to join him as he headed toward the chairs near the ash-encrusted hearth.

"You should not take it personally, my dear," he advised, his blue eyes twinkling. "Men—knights in particular—tend to forget even comely young ladies when their talk strays to their work."

"I do not take it personally! I do not care one whit what Lucien does or whom he goes off with, be it Hubert or some princess from another land! In truth," she added sourly, "I wish he'd go off to some other land."

Osric smothered a smile. "You protest too vehemently, Adrienne. Methinks you care a great deal about your old friend."

"Old—!" Clutching the arms of her chair, she nearly leaped up and almost told Osric the truth. But her sense of self-preservation prevailed and she, too, restrained an impulse. "I—I beg to differ, my lord. I'd not seen Lucien for many years, and I doubt I gave him a thought the entire time. I care no more about him now."

"No?" Leaning toward Adrienne, he rested his elbow on the chair's arm and cupped his chin in his hand. "I would have wagered there was something between you two."

She felt her cheeks flushing ruddily and turned away. "You'd have lost the wager, Grandfather."

"Then you've no interest in Sir Lucien . . . mayhap as a husband?"

"A husband!" Adrienne shrieked, no longer able to remain sitting. She rounded on Osric and hovered over him. "You and Lottie. You must both be drinking from the same cup."

"Your sister thinks as I do?"

Adrienne nodded. " 'Tis a good thing this is no game of chance. You'd both have lost a few silver coins." Taking a deep breath and throwing back her shoulders, she said, "I thought you had men in mind who would make good husbands for Lottie and me. You weren't beginning to consider Lucien, too?"

Osric shrugged. "I have two granddaughters, and Wilfred can only marry one of you. I thought, perhaps, if you and the young knight were fond of each other . . ." He shrugged again.

"We are not." Adrienne sat down hard in the chair beside Osric. "I'm afraid you'll have to find some other lord to wed me."

"That shouldn't be too difficult. Though he would no doubt be considerably older, perhaps less fine to look upon. Mayhap not too virile."

Eyes flying open wide, she stared hard at Osric. "Why—why—how can you speak of such things?" she demanded, her tone hushed.

Osric laughed and patted Adrienne's hand. "My dear, because I am old and long-widowed does not mean I cannot remember what it is to be newly wed. The marriage bed plays a large part in a couple's early union. Some women can be content with husbands who are not too demanding. You, I think, would not be content. Besides," he added quickly, before Adrienne could comment, "I hope to have grandsons through you and Charlotte, one of whom will someday inherit Eynsham."

"Certainly your friend, Lord Wilfred, hopes to sire that child."

"Aye." Osric's eyes narrowed. "Is it you who wish to bear it for him?"

"Nay!" The protest exploded from her lips, embarrassing her for nearly having revealed her intense dislike of her guardian's good friend. " 'Tis Lottie who may be taken with him."

Two bushy eyebrows shot up. "That's good news. I—"

The sound of hurried footsteps caused Osric to pause. Turning to look toward the arched entryway nearest the keep's front portal, he and Adrienne spied Charlotte rushing in.

"Charlotte," Osric said to her. "Is something amiss, that both my granddaughters return without the escorts they left with?"

He smiled, but Charlotte, breathless and disheveled, did not appear to detect the levity in his tone. "I, uh . . ." she stammered, taking a quick, deep breath. "He—Lord Wilfred—is . . . not far behind." Her dark eyes sought Adrienne's.

And Adrienne felt a stab of concern. "Are you well?" she asked, hurrying toward her.

"Yes, I am well."

By the time she reached Charlotte, Adrienne could see the bits of grass stuck to her clothes and that the veil she'd worn anchored to her hair was now missing. "What happened?"

"Nothing," a masculine voice responded.

Adrienne looked up and Charlotte turned; they spied Wilfred leaning against the arch.

He smiled at them and Osric, too. Yet his eyes locked on Charlotte's as he explained, "The lady had a mishap. She fell off her palfrey."

"Is that true?" Adrienne demanded of her sister.

"Are you certain you're unhurt?" Osric inquired with concern as he levered himself out of his chair and strode toward the girls.

"It is true, and I am not hurt, I assure you," Charlotte

vowed. " 'Twas a silly thing. We were riding only at a walk when my mount stumbled, going down on her forelegs. It—it caught me unaware, and I lost my balance. I feel foolish," she muttered as she lowered her head.

"There's no need for shame, my dear," Osric told her, patting her shoulder comfortingly. " 'Even the most expert rider can take a fall."

"And I am no expert rider," she declared, her head coming up again. "Ask Adrienne. She knows."

Before she thought better of it, Adrienne argued, "I would not say that. True, you did little riding while at the nunnery, but you always rode when we were children. I think you are a fine rider."

"I appreciate your high opinion of my equestrian skills, but I must disagree." Charlotte shared another brief glance with Wilfred, who had not moved from his position at the front of the hall. When she looked back at Adrienne, she was frowning. "Did something happen to you?"

"Me?" The younger sister glanced down at her dirty tunics. "Oh, nay. I've been working in my garden, and I've not yet had the opportunity to clean up.

"Let us both go to our chamber now," she suggested. "I can examine you to see if you've any cuts or bruises that need tending, and I can take another bath."

"Excuse us," Charlotte muttered softly, avoiding Wilfred's gaze as she addressed their grandfather. Quickly, she scurried up the stairs with Adrienne.

On the way up the steps, Adrienne requested a tub and hot water from a passing servant. Once inside their shared bedchamber, she immediately washed her hands and ordered Charlotte to sit.

"You needn't do this," Charlotte told her as she sat obediently on the edge of the bed. "Nothing was hurt but my pride."

"If that be true, let me make sure of it. 'Twill make me and Grandfather feel better if I do."

With a reluctant but resigned sigh, Charlotte stood long enough to remove her pretty gowns. Clad only in her smock, she subjected herself to her sister's inspection. Even her head was not spared, as Adrienne gently explored her scalp for lumps and bumps and cuts.

"Oh, Adrienne, stop!" she complained finally. "I told you there is naught." A servant intruding with a knock at their door caused her to add, "Have your bath, now, and leave me be."

Adrienne opened the door and ushered in the servants. As they dragged a tub inside the room and began filling it with buckets of heated water, she watched her sister pull on a robe, hugging it tightly closed over her bosom.

"Lottie, what are you hiding?" she asked softly when the servants had gone again.

"Nothing."

"You are. I glimpsed something on your breast. A discoloring."

Charlotte's face grew warm with an infusion of color.

"Don't be modest with me," Adrienne pleaded. "We've bathed together since I was born."

As she spoke, she moved closer to Charlotte. Now, with two hands, she pulled open the edge of her sister's robe and lowered the neckline of her delicate smock. "A rash?" she wondered aloud, glancing up to meet Charlotte's eyes for confirmation. But Charlotte offered neither that nor a denial; she looked stricken, frantic.

Adrienne looked down again at the plum-colored marks spreading brightly across the swell of her sister's left breast. "Bruises!" she realized aloud. This time when she met Charlotte's eyes, her own were wide with horror. "Lottie, they look to be the marks left by someone's fingers!"

"No doubt they are! My own, left by my hand when I

fell upon it." She wrenched her garments free of Adrienne's light grasp and clutched the edge of her robe closed once again.

"Truly?"

"Truly."

"Then your arm must be sore." Before Charlotte could elude her, Adrienne grabbed her arm, pushed up the sleeve to inspect it more closely, and then proceeded to bend it vigorously at the elbow, up and down, up and down.

"Of course it's sore," Charlotte ground out, again pulling herself free. "And your pumping it as if it were a forge bellows is not helping in the least!"

Adrienne's concerns had grown into suspicions. Now she felt guilty. Charlotte would never lie of her own volition; she should have taken her at her word.

"I'm sorry. I'll have my bath and leave you be. Rest now. We've some time before supper."

With a silent nod, Charlotte took to bed while Adrienne stripped off her dirty clothes and climbed into the bath. Yet when it was time to go down for the evening meal, Charlotte declined, claiming new aches had caught up with her. Adrienne took to the stairs alone.

Lucien returned to the keep the way he had left it, through the kitchen. He felt in fine spirits, better than any he could recall since he'd last left Eynsham Keep. Not only had Hubert obliged him with a thorough tour and explanation of Osric's defenses, Lucien now realized there was a way for him to have Addy—not just for another fleeting, secret tryst, but forever as his wife. And having Adrienne of Eynsham as his lawful lady wife would be as fortuitous for himself as it had been for Henry of Anjou when he took Eleanor of Aquitaine as his bride.

Lucien's belly rumbled. He'd had nothing to eat since he'd broken his fast that morning. The smells accosting him now as he stepped into the scullery made his stomach cramp in anticipation.

"Ach! 'Scuse me, milord," the rotund cook begged as her enormous backside bumped into him. She set the succulent leg of lamb she had just taken from the fire onto a platter. "I didna' know you were behind me."

"It was my fault." He bowed slightly at the waist as he tried to figure how he knew her. She had not been Eynsham's chief cook under his mother's eye. Nay, but . . . Suddenly it came to him. She was Hilda, a plump lass when he had last seen her in Evandale. And that was the reason he remembered her, for Hilda had been the only plump, apparently well-fed, villager during Gundulf's days.

"Done to perfection," he noted, referring to the meat. "I don't know if I can wait until it's set out on the table."

"You hungry, milord?" she asked, and he nodded. "Well, sit yerself down there, if you will, and I'll bring you a bite to hold you over. Supper won't be served for a while, yet."

Readily, Lucien perched on a high stool near the work table. The woman who ruled the kitchen wiped her fingers on her tunic as she barked orders to the scullions scurrying about, doing her bidding. It was she, though, who personally filled a trencher for him.

Eagerly he dove into it, his fingers grasping what his eating knife did not spear. The hollowed bread loaf was heaped full of roasted duckling in gravy, sweet peas, and glazed pears. Beside it Hilda set a heel of fresh bread with a small pot of honey to spread over it.

The cook hovered over Lucien, watching intently as he ate each bite. Still chewing, he grinned up at her. "The best, mistress. Better even than what any of King Henry's cooks serve up!"

"Yer in service to our king, are you?" She seemed impressed when Lucien nodded. "My name is Hilda, milord," she announced, bobbing a quick curtsy that made her huge breasts jiggle while threatening to offset her balance.

Lucien might have chuckled at her effort if he hadn't feared her going over and landing with her feet in the air. "No need to be so formal, mistress. Ah, Hilda."

She grinned at him, her cheeks rosy from the exertion and the heat of the cookfires. "Would you like a fruit pastry t' go with that? I've got some fine gooseberry tarts. Oh, and some ale. What have I been thinkin'?"

Before he could say yea or nay, she was off. When Hilda returned with a mug of ale and a tart smothered in thick, clotted cream, he thanked her.

"I am called Lucien," he added.

"Sir Lucien." She plucked at her skirts again, preparing to bounce another bow. But Lucien reached out and grabbed her wrist.

"Nay. No more curtsying to me, I pray you. I'm just a humble visitor to your lord's keep."

"Come to wed one o' the ladies, did you?" she asked slyly.

Lucien stopped chewing the mass of berries and cream he had just put into his mouth. When he swallowed it all down, he tossed back a swig of ale and wiped the foam from his lips. "What makes you think that?"

"Am I talkin' out o' turn?"

"No, no. I'm just curious."

"Oh." The cook heaved her girth onto a nearby stool. " 'Tis only that it's all the talk 'round the keep, that Lord Osric is bringing in suitors fer the ladies. He thinks it high time they be wed, y' know."

"Really?"

"Oh, aye. He brought that Lord Wilfred here to look 'em over, that be the truth."

His smile faded as a frown creased his brow. "Lord Wilfred. Yes. I'd forgotten that seemed to be the reason for his being here."

"I was only thinkin '," Hilda continued, "that you might be here to consider Lady Charlotte as yer bride."

"Lady Charlotte! Why not Lady Adrienne?"

"Oh, milord!" Hilda fanned her expansive bosom with her chubby hand. "Lady Charlotte wouldna' survive bein' wed to the likes o' Wilfred o' Houghton." She leaned on the table with one elbow, bringing her face closer to Lucien's. Lowering her voice to a whisper, she said, "You did say I'm not speakin' out 'o turn."

"You're not."

"Well, he's too old and too worldly and too everythin' for our Lady Charlotte. Even if he never took a hand to her, he'd bully her 'til he broke her, which would be no time a'tall."

"Why do you think that?"

Hilda pulled a face. "Well, she may be the eldest o' the sisters, but by less than a twelve-month, as I understand it. And she be so quiet and demure and refined . . ."

Lucien arched one eyebrow and leveled an emerald eye at Hilda. "Are you saying, mistress, that Lady Adrienne is not?"

"Nay!" She punctuated her protest with a shake of her head. "But Lady Charlotte's timid, she is, while Lady Adrienne, well, she's not! You yerself know she had them runnin' off to Carrington Fair when the old lord's back was turned. She's always off and about, that one. She goes to Evandale quite a bit, tendin' the villagers—and the servants here, too, for that matter—when they're ailin' or wounded. She helped birth Cecil and Audrey's last babe, as if she were chatelaine o' the keep! An' she don't just birth the villagers' babes, oh, nay. She'll stick her arms in a mare up to her elbows to pull out a foal.

"Lady Charlotte, now, holds close to home," Hilda continued. "She does her weavin' and sewin' in the solar, and she reads her scriptures all the time and says her prayers. In truth, the only thing that draws Lady Charlotte t' the town is the church there, and Father Lawrence. She was goin' t' be a nun, you know. Only reason she isn't now is, since their parents died o' the pox, Lord Osric wants 'em both wed."

Hilda blinked her thin-lashed eyes and gave Lucien an apologetic smile. "What I mean to be sayin'," she whispered confidentially, "is we all think Lady Adrienne could hold her own married to the likes o' Lord Wilfred. An' we none of us, the servants that is, think Lady Charlotte is up t' the task."

For a long minute Lucien absorbed this information. "What do you think Lord Osric's feelings are on this matter?"

"Well, he's no fool, our lord isn't. So he must be leanin' toward his old friend weddin' Lady Adrienne, and then findin' another t' wed the girl's sister." She bobbed her head so that her triple chins quivered. "Some of us were just hopin' you might be the one fer Lady Charlotte."

Lucien blinked slowly, a gesture that implied his understanding rather than a confirmation of the cook's—the staff's—hopes. Yet he said nothing more, so Hilda excused herself, waddling away to supervise the preparation of the rest of the evening's meal. Lucien caught the woman staring at him from far corners of the room, but he ignored her glances as he concentrated on finishing his ale.

His cup had just been emptied when Hilda returned to the table. "Would you like another mugful?"

Lucien nodded, and she poured. "If I might risk bein'

bold again, milord, I have the oddest feelin' I've seen you before.''

He stiffened, keeping his eyes on the cup as Hilda filled it to the brim with amber brew. "I think not," he said evenly.

"You never visited Eynsham before, nor Evandale either?" she pressed. He denied it with a shake of his head. "Well, I guess I've not seen you, then. But I know I've seen someone who looks like you." She hugged the pitcher to her breasts as she turned. "It'll come to me who," Lucien heard her say as she walked away. "If I ponder on it a bit, it'll come."

Alone at the table, he drained his cup with a few quick swallows. Time was shorter than he'd thought, he realized. If Osric were planning to wed Addy off to Wilfred, and if Hilda put her mind to it and remembered who he really was, he'd not only lose his advantage, he might not live to wage the battle that could win him back his keep.

He had to put the spur to the steed, he decided, rising and heading toward the door that linked the kitchen with the hall. The first thing he needed to do was to wed Addy.

Chapter 13

Lucien strode into the great hall just as the last of the trestle tables was set up for Osric's men-at-arms. He found the old man and his erstwhile comrade, Wilfred, seated as they often were, together in two chairs at the center of the dais table.

"Join us," Osric urged companionably when he spied Lucien. "How did you enjoy your tour of the keep?"

"Alas," he returned dryly, taking a chair opposite, "I've yet to look into a single chamber except for the room you so kindly offered for my use."

"Adrienne told me you were busy with Hubert. How do you find things here at Eynsham?"

Lucien eyed his foe critically, the distorted version of the truth Osric had told Adrienne flaring brightly in his mind. Yet he admitted grudgingly to the one who sat in *his* chair presiding over *his* lands, "Well ordered. Your knights seem well enough prepared to follow you on cru-